BLOODY UNION

BOOK 1 IN THE MADE SERIES

BROOKE SUMMERS

Copyright

First Edition published in 2020
   Text Copyright © Brooke Summers
   All rights reserved. The moral right of the author has been asserted.

Cover Design by Under Cover Designs.
   Formatter Author Bunnies.
   Editing by Edits By Erin.
   Proofread by Author Bunnies.

No part of this publication may be reproduced, stored in or introduced into a retrieval system, or transmitted, in any form or by any means (electronic, mechanical, photocopying, recording or otherwise), nor be otherwise circulated in any form of binding or cover other than that in which it is published without the prior written permission of the author. Any person who does any unauthorized act in relation to this publication may be liable to criminal prosecution and civil claims for damages.

All characters in this publication are fictitious and any resemblance to real persons, living or dead, is purely coincidental.

Books by Brooke:

Forbidden Lust

Dangerous Secrets

Forever Love

The Made Series:

Bloody Union

Unexpected Union

Standalones:

Saving Reli

For Erin

There's not enough words to say how very lucky I am to have you in my life. Not only an amazing editor, but also my friend.

Prologue

Makenna

THERE'S a slight tremble to my hands but I try hiding it. The Famiglia are in my father's office, the Capo sits in front of my father. His son, the Capo Bastone sits beside him, while his brothers stand behind them, all of them tense and ready to start killing if need be.

The darkening of Dante's eyes tells me that he's seen my hands tremble. My breath hitches as I take in his gorgeous green eyes, the sadistic grin and the dark stubble that surrounds it. "Makenna," he says and I raise my eyes to his.

"Makenna..." my father says and I turn my gaze to him. His tone is harsher than it usually is with me and I know that it's due to the men that are sitting in his office. My father is head of the Ceannaire ar chách, the Irish Mafia here in New York. He has been since my grandfather took a bullet to the heart from the Bratva. He was lucky and survived; I don't know how. Granda says that no way on this earth were the Russian's going to be his downfall. He's living life to the fullest in Dublin, Ireland where he's the head of the Mafia. "Matteo Bianchi..."

My body tenses, I hate the Capo, have since I was twelve years old.

Nobody knows about my hatred of Matteo and no one ever will. I know the consequences of what will happen if anyone finds out the truth about that night.

My father carries on talking, "And I have agreed that our families being bonded is the only way to guarantee peace." I hide the scoff, this is absolute bullshit, there's no way that anything can be guaranteed. It'll be put on hold for a while, but something is bound to piss one of them off at some stage and then all hell will break loose. "You and Dante will marry."

I grit my teeth, I knew one day I'd have to marry, it's the way our world works. A woman in the Mafia doesn't have the life like a normal woman, we're to be seen and not heard. We're to be at the beck and call of our father and then our husband. I've been lucky, my father isn't a monster to his family, unlike some of his men. From what I've heard most of the *made men* beat their women and children to submit to their wishes. Break the woman so they won't disobey them.

I take a deep breath. "Yes, father." My gaze moves to my brothers who are standing in the corner of the office, they are looking at me with a weird expression. Did they think I'd object? I've not got a death wish. I'm not stupid. I'd never disrespect my father, not in front of his men and definitely not in front of men that are our enemies.

My father nods his head, "You are fourteen, Makenna, and the wedding will take place when you are of age." His tone is darker once again, this isn't for my benefit, this is for the Famiglia.

"Of course," Dante says harshly.

Matteo shakes his head, "As soon as you're of age, we'll have the wedding." He turns his gaze to me, "You can go."

My brothers tense, their hands on their guns, all of them eager to be the one to shoot him. There's no love lost there and the tension in the room becomes thick.

"Makenna, go to your mother." My father demands and I hold back the protest. I give my brothers a smile as I leave the office.

My mother is waiting for me in the living room. Her hands by her side and a smile on her face. She rushes over to me. "You're finally getting married," she says and to anyone else it would be as though she's congratulating me. To me, I know better, she's been waiting for this day for a long time. Waiting for me to leave the house where she knows that the secret I carry will no longer risk being spilled.

ONE

Dante
___

THE LOOKS I get as I walk into the bar are nothing unusual. The women's eyes are full of arousal, want and fear and the men's are either full of fear and respect, or fear and hatred. It's always been like this, since I was twelve, when I had my first kill. The fucker had it coming, he had his knife to my mother's neck, by the time my bullet had entered the asshole's head my mother had her throat slit. The next day, I became a *made man*.

"Dante," Alessio my youngest brother growls and I smirk when I see three of the Irish Mafia men sitting at the bar. "Fucking hate those Irish bastards."

"We're at peace now," I tell him, even though I'd love nothing more than to put a fucking bullet in their brains.

He scoffs, "Please don't tell me you believe that shit."

Of fucking course I don't. "Do I look like I'm stupid?"

He laughs, "No, but then again, you're marrying the Gallagher girl."

The mention of her name has my gut tightening. I've not seen her in five years. Seamus Gallagher, the Ceannaire ar chách, the head of the Irish Mafia here in New

York, thinks he's the leader of all; hell, he's not even the leader of New York. That would be us. He's managed to keep his daughter out of all the rags and newspapers. Not a fucking picture of her anywhere, not even online. I feel like I'm walking in blind.

"I am."

Tomorrow I'll see her again, and in three days, we'll be married. Fuck.

One of the Irish men lifts their cell to their ear, not once have they taken their eyes off of me. I smirk, I don't give a fuck if they're on edge that we're here. When he puts his cell in his pocket I raise my brow, "What's the matter, boys?" I grin as their bodies tense. "We're going to be family soon." I'm taunting them and they fall into the trap, their fingers edging closer to their guns. "Reach for them and I'll rip your fucking heads off." I grit as I walk toward them. Their eyes narrow, but they're not quick enough to hide the fear that seeps into them. I know they see the demons that lurk in my eyes, the darkness that stalks my heels. It's a darkness that wouldn't have me hesitating to kill each and every one of them, and I'd do it without remorse.

"We're here for a drink, not to kill you." The threat of 'yet' hangs in the air as Seamus walks up behind me.

"You'll not be harmed while you're in my establishment." His Irish brogue is thick as he walks over to his three men. "Why aren't you at the airport?"

They straighten their backs, the respect shining in their eyes. "Boss, she told us that she wasn't arriving until morning."

Seamus narrows his eyes, "Finish your drinks, we're leaving."

They're instantly on edge, something is going on and I'm not sure what.

"Need any help?" I ask quietly and Seamus grins. "I'll take that as a no. But if you change your mind, you've got my number."

He nods, "I'll see you tomorrow, Dante." Just as I thought, he wouldn't ever accept my help. It would be seen as weak. "Enjoy your evening." There's a reproach in his voice, is he warning me to behave? I grin darkly at him, I'm not a man who can be controlled. I'll do whatever the fuck I want, whenever the fuck I want.

Romero slides beside me, his face deadpan but I know him, he's boiling with rage as we watch the Irish leave.

"Not now," I warn him.

"It'll be a bloody wedding yet." He grins.

There's not been a bloody wedding in the Famiglia for over a decade. "They won't start a war, not at a wedding."

He raises a brow, "You sure about that?"

I glare at him, of course I'm not fucking sure. But they'd be dead by the end of it. "Fuck, I need a drink."

"You need to get your dick wet."

I grit my teeth, trying not to kill my brother.

"You never know when to shut the fuck up do you, Romero?" Alessio grins.

Romero shrugs, "I'm going to die someday."

I ignore their stupidity and turn my eyes to the women that are around the bar, some have their heads down, others giving me the fuck me eyes. None of them hold my attention for very long.

Romero lets out a low whistle. "Fucking finally," he mutters and my gaze follows his where two women have just walked into the bar. There's a busty brunette who's wearing a tight pink dress and matching heels, but it's her friend that I'll be fucking by the end of the night. Black leather pants look as though they've been painted onto her, black boots that reach her knee and a red fucking top that clings to every curve of her body. Her blonde hair is curled, falling around her neck and down past her breasts. Both walk in as though they own the place, heads held high as they saunter toward the bar. The barman's eyes widen but he serves them.

They find a corner in the bar and stay there, the girls don't care about the appreciative looks that they're getting. Not once have they glanced around the bar to see who's here. Fucking stupid.

"How the hell are they not surrounded by now?" Alessio muses and I agree, not that I'd admit it. They've been left alone even though their beauty by far outshines any other women.

The night wears on and the women haven't so much as looked at anyone in the bar. It's pissing Romero off that they haven't glanced at him, he wants the brunette.

My hand reaches for my gun when I hear a man growl, "Bitch!" Three fucking Russians stalk toward the women. I'm slightly impressed that both women stand and glare at the Bratva bastards. Fucking hell, they have a death wish.

One of the Russians backhand the brunette viciously making her fall backward to the floor. The blonde woman steps forward and raises her brow. Jesus Christ. The hum of bikes is in the far distance. I watch as she tells the Russian that he's a dead man, before one of the other Russians punches her in the ribs, knocking the breath from her lungs. She doesn't back down, she stands tall and glares at the Russians.

Alessio, Romero, and I get to our feet, I notice the barman is tense, his eyes on the girls. The rumble of bikes grow closer, they're outside. Within seconds, eight fucking bikers walk in. The women sigh and turn to the door where the bikers have their eyes on them, the blonde steps back, whereas the brunette takes a step toward them.

"Which one?" the biker asks and the brunette smirks as she slides her eyes to the guy that backhanded her. "Time for you to go home," he tells her and she nods, the blonde steps toward her and they walk past us. One of the bikers grabs a hold of the blonde's arm and pulls her toward him. "You good?" he asks, his eyes taking her in and for some reason I want to rip his fucking hand of her.

She steps out of his hold. "No worries, Ace, I'm grand," she says with her thick velvety Irish accent.

"You sure."

She nods. "Positive."

The biker regards her closely, "Time for you to go on home." I can't make out the blonde's reaction to his demand but I see the smirk on his face. "Before your brothers catch you here."

Her bell like laughter rings out and I feel it in my gut. What the fuck is going on? "Come on, Kinsley," the blonde laughs, "before your brother starts to lecture us."

The biker grins as the girls leave the bar. His eyes narrow in on me, a warning in his eyes. He nods to his brothers and they pick up the asshole that backhanded his sister and the other two fuckers that are with him.

"What the fuck was that about?" Romero asks as he makes his way out of the bar behind the bikers.

I have no fucking idea.

"Are you ready for this?" Romero asks and I glare at him.

"Of course he's ready," my father says and I shift my glare to him, unlike my brother he doesn't back down. "War between the families has been going on for decades, this wedding is finally a way to bring peace." It's a warning. He's telling me not to fuck up.

"I know my duty, Father," I say through clenched teeth.

"The wedding is in three days, Dante. One mistake and we'll pay dearly."

I don't answer him, instead I keep my gaze firmly in front of me. Seamus, Finn, Patrick, and Cian Gallagher stand at their door, all of their eyes on us. Seamus glares at my father, whereas the Gallagher brother's death glares are aimed at me.

"Do they really think they can out shoot us?" Alessio comments as he takes in the guards that surround the monstrosity of the Gallagher Mansion. The Fucking Irish don't do things small by any means. They're flashy assholes.

Our father gives Alessio a harsh look, we've seen that look a thousand times. It doesn't work on any of us. Not anymore. "Enough of your shit," he demands.

We walk toward the Gallagher's, none of us are happy about this but right now, we've got to deal with it. "Gentleman," Seamus calls out and I grit my teeth.

"Where is she?" My father asks, with a bite to his tone.

Christ.

"She'll be here soon. Right now, we've got some things to iron out." Seamus' eyes are hard as he glares at my father.

As Capo, my father leads. I, as his capo bastone, or Underboss as most call it, follow. Although, if I have anything to say about it, Romero will be my capo bastone when I become the Capo. My father's time has come to an end and it's only a matter of time before he meets his. My father is a monster, we all are; it's who we are. But unlike my father, I'm not a fucking monster to those closest to me.

I protect those that are and retaliate against those that hurt them.

My father nods, that's his signal that we're to follow the Gallagher's into the lion's den. My father first, followed closely behind by me and then my brothers, our men hidden around the perimeter of the Gallagher mansion. Seamus and his sons lead us toward his office. I haven't been here since we agreed that I'd marry his only daughter, Makenna. She was fourteen when I last saw her, over five years ago. She was small and scrawny, pretty in an innocent way but I didn't pay too much attention. I'm not into kids and Makenna certainly was a child. I'm curious to see how she's changed.

Seamus opens the door to his office and I see that nothing's changed since I was here last. The huge mahogany desk takes up half the fucking office. Yet again, it makes me wonder why they have to try and be so flashy, are they trying to make up for something?

My father takes a seat and I take the one beside him, both my brothers and the Gallagher brothers continue to stand.

"This is a waste of our time," my father grits out. We had come under the impression that we'd be seeing Makenna today, instead, we're going into his office to fucking chitchat.

"My daughter's well-being—" Seamus begins, "—is not a waste of time," he growls. This is the first time that I've seen this side to him. Usually he's calm and composed. Sitting across from me now isn't the Ceannaire ar chách, instead he's a dangerous man who's determined to make sure that I look after his daughter.

This should be fun.

"Are you trying to insinuate that my son won't be a gentleman?"

I glance to my side where Romero is standing, a smile tugging on his lips. My name and the words gentleman don't belong in the same sentence. I'm anything but, and if Seamus thinks telling his daughter that will help, he's sorely fucking mistaken.

"Like Dante knows what being a gentleman consists of," Finn growls.

These men are playing a dangerous game, they've shown us their ultimate weakness and by doing so, they've shown us where to target them if need be.

"You have something to say?" I ask with a raised brow.

Seamus regards my father first and that pisses me the fuck off. I'm a grown ass man, one that has killed hundreds of men, my name is feared by everyone and yet I'm ignored because my father's the capo. My father nods, and Seamus turns his gaze to me.

"My daughter is—" He pauses if to find the right word. "Unique," he says with a glare at me.

"Difficult," Cian says and I see the loving smile on his face.

"A pain in the ass." Patrick grins.

"A fucking princess," Finn replies darkly and that right there is a threat.

"I can handle a woman."

The look the Gallagher's give me would make a grown man quiver, but not me, I stare them down.

"Fuck, you're as stubborn as she is," Seamus says and the grin on his face makes me brace for what he's about to say next. "You two are going to be a match made in fucking hell."

"Is that all?" my father asks. "I'd like to see the girl now."

I grit my teeth, that fucking look in his eye is enough to tell me why he wants to see Makenna. Asshole.

Seamus narrows his eyes at my father, but stands. I hear a door opening and Seamus grins. "She's here." He walks out of his office and we all follow. "Makenna," he calls out and I hear the sound of heels clicking against the floor.

As we enter the sitting room, my gaze follows the Gallagher's.

"Shit," Romero curses.

"Holy shit," Alessio mutters.

Standing in front of us is Makenna, the blonde from the bar. She's wearing a tight tank top and even tighter fucking jeans, her hair tied up into a slick ponytail, there's not an ounce of makeup on her face. She's fucking gorgeous, but if the narrowing of her eyes is anything to go by, she's going to be defiant.

My anger begins to rise as I remember the punch she took a few nights ago. She has her arms crossed over her chest and stares at her father. Yet again she's not looking at me or my family, just as she did in the bar.

"I'd like to have a talk with my Fiancée alone." I contain my bubbling anger from the glares of her family but I just stare them down.

Seamus glares at me but nods and he and his son's leave, my father and brothers following behind. I turn my attention to Makenna once the door is closed behind them. "Show me," I growl, needing to see the damage.

She raises her brow at me, the defiance clear in her eyes. I take a step closer to her. She's not intimidated by me, I can tell as she holds her head high. She's changed a lot from the fourteen year old who trembled when she was in a room full of *made men*. Now, she stares me in the eye. She's good, not showing any fear.

"Lift your top and let me see," I growl.

She doesn't even bat an eyelid. "And why should I do that?"

My mouth goes to her ear, "I watched that man punch you, Makenna. I want to see the damage."

She steps back and lifts her shirt, a black bruise mars her creamy skin. "Happy now?"

I grit my teeth, "Ecstatic."

"It's nice to know that my husband-to-be watches as a man hits me." She takes another step backward. "Guess what they say is true, hmm? The Famiglia really know how to treat a woman."

I reach for her and pull her toward me. "I will not raise a hand to you. Ever."

She looks at me and I see the scepticism in her eyes, see the disbelief clear as day, but she doesn't answer. My fingers caress her bruise and she winces before closing her eyes. When she opens them again, they're clear, but unreadable. I don't like that she's a closed book to me. Damn, the Gallagher's have taught her well. I'm going to find the man that hit her and gut him like the fucking animal he is. She pulls down her top and looks at me, curiosity in her eyes.

I take a step closer to her and watch as she gulps, fear creeping into her eyes. "Make no mistake, Makenna, I am the Underboss of the Famiglia and you'll give me the respect that I have earned," I say through clenched teeth; that fucking fear has no place between us, but at the same time, she needs to realize who I am.

I reach into my pocket, and pull out the ring that had been in there since yesterday. I place it on her finger, loving the way her eyes widen as I touch her hand. "Three days and then your mine." I step back before I do something stupid like fucking kiss her. Once I do that, I'm going to fuck her until she passes out.

Makenna's eyes flash with heat and indignation, before she's able to say anything the door opens. She turns to see who's there and that's when I spot the white raised scar at the base of her throat.

I know what that scar means.

What the fuck happened to her and who the fuck did it to her?

TWO

Dante

SEAMUS WALKS in and glances between me and his daughter, his eyes like a fucking hawk as he spots the diamond ring on her finger. He gives me a nod and I understand. I give Makenna one more glance before I leave and pull the door behind me. I don't close it fully as he intended, instead, I leave it open slightly so that I can hear what's being said. "Makenna?" His voice is fucking soft. This is why he didn't want me in the room with them

She gives him a smile and that fucking smile hits me in the gut. What the hell is wrong with me? She's a woman; I've had countless over the years and yet this one makes me fucking lose my head. "Yeah, da?" Just as her father's was, her voice is soft and gentle. It's clear to see that they have a lot of love for each other.

"Behave tonight." He warns her and I watch as she bites her lip trying to stifle her laughter. "Makenna…" He glances at the door but I stay hidden. "Matteo is…"

Her eyes flash with pure hatred for my father, something I hadn't thought I'd see from anyone but me and my brothers. "I know, da, don't worry."

Seamus shakes his head. "You'll be the death of me, Kenna, I swear to God, you'll put me in an early grave."

She cocks her brow, "Early would have been twenty years ago, da."

I tamper down the smile. Fuck, she's a smartass.

"Thank fuck you're out of my hair soon." There's no heat in his words but I see the hurt flash through Makenna's eyes. "Does your mom know you're here?"

The pure hatred that flashed through her features at the mention of my father's name is nothing in comparison to what she has at the mention of her mom, she looks as though she wants to kill her. "Nope, but I guess you'll tell her."

Seamus sighs, as he gets to his feet he pulls her into his arms. The softness he has for her is definitely his weakness; if he shows this to anyone they'd use it against him. They'd hurt Makenna just to hurt him.

She pulls out of her father's arms, "I'll go find *mother.*" The way she spits out the word makes me wonder what the hell happened between her and her mom, she walks toward a different door and leaves, slamming it shut behind her.

"I should kill you for listening in on the conversation," Seamus tells me as I walk into the room again, where he's glaring at me. "Did you get what you wanted?"

I glare back at him. "Seamus," I say, my tone serious. "What happened to her?"

He sighs, "Fuck knows." He mutters, "Was attending to some fucking animal, and got a call from Finn. He'd just returned home to find Kenna on the floor beaten and bleeding out." His voice breaks, he's unable to talk. I leave him be for a moment, letting him get his composure back. My blood is boiling, my hands balled into fists. "Someone slit her throat, luckily we found her in time. Haven't found out who did it yet. But when I do, I'm going to carve them like a fucking pumpkin."

I nod, "I'll be there when you do it." Seamus looks at me in shock. Fuck, this woman is getting to me and I have no idea why. "She's going to be my wife."

He looks at me with respect, "Okay."

"How old was she?"

He shakes his head again, his eyes dark and I can see the storm raging in them. "She was twelve."

Fucking hell.

"When she was released from hospital, I sent her to stay with my brother," he informs me. He wanted her safe, so he sent her away. I'd have done the same thing. It also explains why her accent is thicker than her brother's, she sounds like her father.

"Your father is an arsehole, Dante." I glare at him, he's treading a fucking thin line right now. "It's true, we both know it. The only reason I agreed to this fucking shit was because of you."

I raise my brow in confusion.

"You think I haven't looked into you, into your family?" He snarls at me, "I have, I know exactly who your father is. I know what he does to girls like my daughter. Do you honestly think I'd have let her marry you if you were just like him?"

I laugh, it's bitter and cold. "You have no idea what I'm like. I'm worse than my father."

He nods, "That maybe so, boyo, but you're not a fucking arsehole to women like your father is."

I tense at him calling me boyo. What the fuck am I, five?

"She's my daughter. I want peace between us. But I will go to war with you if my daughter gets hurt."

"She's going to be my wife," I repeat my earlier words.

He stares at me in disgust. "You're forgetting something," he snaps taking a step toward me, his voice low and bristling with anger. "I watched your mother wither away under the beatings she took from your father. I won't sit back and let that happen to my daughter."

I step up to him so we're face to face. My body is tight with my unleashed anger. He's lucky, I haven't broken his jaw. No one speaks to me like Seamus has and gets away with it. "I am not my father. I will not lay a hand on my wife in anger." I say through gritted teeth. "Let me make myself extremely clear, Makenna is going to be my wife, she's mine."

He takes a step back, a slow smile sneaking across his lips. "Okay then." He turns and walks out of the room, leaving me wondering what the fuck is wrong with the man?

It doesn't take me long to catch up to him and we walk into the dining room where everyone is sitting waiting for us. Makenna's sitting beside Finn, an empty seat beside her and another empty seat at the top of the table. I walk over and sit beside Makenna, she's glaring at her mom who's looking down at her hands. My father has his sadistic grin on his face, loving the way things are tense.

Mrs Gallagher clicks her fingers and the maids come in carrying the food.

"That's a nasty scar you have." My father grins as he leers at Makenna.

I watch as she grips her knife, her eyes full of hate, she looks as though she's dying to kill the bastard. Her mother gasps and covers her mouth with a shaky hand. I turn my gaze to my brother's, they both have no expression on their faces, almost as if they haven't noticed but I know they have. There will be questions later and I'll get my fucking answers.

"Is Killian coming to the wedding?" Finn asks and I notice that Makenna sits up taller, the hand that was gripped around the knife loosens, she's relaxed. Her mother on the other hand looks as though she's about to faint.

Seamus grins, "He should be arriving in the next couple of days."

"Killian?" I ask knowing damn well who they're talking about, I turn to Makenna in time to see that she's giving me a warm smile.

"He's my brother," Seamus says but the way the Gallagher brothers are glancing at one another, there's a hell of a lot more than him being Seamus' brother. I need Orion to look into this shit, one fucking thing I hate is being in a situation where I'm going in blind.

Makenna's attention is on her cell phone. I glance down and see the message from someone called Kinsley. From all the intel I gathered, Kinsley is her best friend and has been since she was a child.

KINSLEY: PARTY TONIGHT?

I GRIT MY TEETH REMEMBERING WHAT HAPPENED THE LAST time she went out. I see her reply saying that she can't, but will ring her later. Kinsley Anderson is the only daughter of Julian 'Jaws' Montry, the president of the Fury Vipers Motorcycle club. They're fucking animals who party hard and kill harder. They're ruthless, and have no loyalty to anyone but the Fury Vipers brothers. They'll do whatever the hell they want and don't care about the consequences. Much like the la Famiglia, they're feared by most. Whereas, we keep a low profile and have businesses as fronts and are fucking gentleman in the presence of the public. Those animals couldn't give a fuck. I know that when Makenna and I are married, I'll be putting a stop to her going to that damn club house.

The dinner is quiet, Mrs Gallagher keeps glancing at Makenna as though she's waiting for her to lose her damn mind. Something about this family doesn't sit right. The hatred that my brothers and I have for my father isn't publicized, we don't want the fucking world knowing that when my father goes down, it could be, and probably will be at our hands. The Famiglia won't allow me to become Capo dei Capi if I've killed the previous one. Hell, it's against our oath to kill another *made man*, but fuck, I've broken that oath before and I'd happily do it again if the fucker needs to be put down. Traitors are different, as soon as they become rats, their *made men* status dies, and they'll soon follow after we torture the fuck out of them to extract as much information as we can. Whereas, Makenna's open hatred for her mom is something I can't understand. I've witnessed the way she is with her father. They have a great relationship, she has a lot of love for him along with her brothers; her eyes soften whenever they talk to her. But it's very different when her mom talks to her, the features on her face harden and she glares at her.

"Mrs Gallagher," my Father says once the dinner is finished, and I watch as she bows her head, "thank you for a wonderful dinner."

The woman gets to her feet, "It was a pleasure to have you." She practically curtsies as she walks backward to exit the room.

"Seamus, I ensure that everything will be ready for the wedding in three days." The harshness to my father's tone has the Gallagher men's hands twitching for their guns.

"Matteo," Seamus glares at him. "What do you take me for?"

"And her…" my father continues, not knowing when to shut his fucking mouth. "She's pure?"

Makenna smirks, not what I'd expect from her. Most woman in our life are untouched, when men talk about sex, they blush and bow their heads with embarrassment. Not Makenna, she smirks and her eyes twinkle. "I'm Catholic," is her response, her accent is thick and full of sarcasm.

"That means nothing," my father says in outrage.

Makenna shrugs, the hatred she has for him is making her be disrespectful. She needs to be careful. I reach over and grip her arm, her gaze snaps to me, eyes narrowed, but she raises a perfectly sculpted eyebrow.

"Watch your mouth," I say through clenched teeth. "Respect."

She glares at me for a moment before smiling and I know that whatever is going to come out of her mouth isn't going to be good. "I'm sorry," she snarls. "Don't worry, Dante here will be the only one to defile me." My grip on her arm tightens, does she really believe that I'd do that to her?

My father nods, pleased with her answer. "And I see that she's drinking." His tone is reproachful.

Makenna reaches for the glass of wine that's in front of her and downs it in one swallow. Romero's eyes flash with humor, but his face is void of emotion. Alessio on the other hand, is unable to stop his lips twitching with amusement.

"I'm Irish," Makenna drawls with a smile and her brothers laugh.

"We can handle our drink, Matteo." Seamus grins. "Have no fear, Makenna can and will drink you and your Italian boys under the table anytime she likes."

Why do I think there's a double meaning to this?

Father gets to his feet and my brothers and I do the same. "Seamus," he says as a way of saying goodbye.

I lean down so that my mouth is level with Makenna's ear. "Soon, Makenna," I whisper and enjoy the tiny shudder she has. "Three days and then you're mine."

She gets to her feet, her expression blank. "Oh, Dante," she whispers. "You're in for a surprise."

"No, darling," I return. "You are. You've lived sheltered for so long. When we go home, you're going to find out what it's like to be in our world. Not to mention what it's like to have my cock inside of you."

The sharp intake of breath is all I needed. I walk away from her before I do something stupid like kiss her.

Once we're outside, my father turns to me. "When you wed her, make sure you teach her manners," he sneers and I glare at the fucking bastard. "Damn bitch," he mutters. "I've got a meeting. Pauly is with me," he says talking about his consigliere. "The sooner this wedding is over, the fucking better."

I don't rise to his bait. He's trying to get a rise out of me, wondering if Makenna has gotten to me. My father believes that a woman is a man's downfall. That all they're good for is fucking and baring our children. While my father is a monster to his women, I on the other hand won't hurt my wife; although I do agree that love is for fools.

"Good," he says, whatever he saw on my face or didn't satisfied him. "You've three days, Dante. Three days before you take that fucking bitch to become your wife." He turns and goes to his car. I stay where I am and watch him leave.

"Bro…" Romero says. "I'll fucking take him out."

"Anytime, anywhere," Alessio agrees.

I shake my head. "Not now." But our time will come.

"What the hell is with him and Makenna? I've never seen someone affect him as she does. He wants to rip her head off." Alessio asks and it's what I've been wondering too.

"I don't know, I saw the way they acted. Something has happened and I'm going to find out what." I make my way to our car, needing to get the hell away from the Gallagher's. Makenna is making me lose my damn fucking mind and I'm not even married to her yet.

"What I want to know is what the hell her mom did to her? I've never seen a woman look at their mom with such hatred." Romero chuckles, "That woman should sleep with one eye open from now on."

I frown, "If Makenna was going to kill her mom, I think she'd have done it by now." I slide into the driver's side and wait for Romero and Alessio to climb in. As soon as they do, I drive, needing some distance between me and Makenna.

That just makes Romero chuckle louder. "Oh, dear brother," he tuts. "I wasn't talking about Makenna, I doubt she can hurt anyone. I'm talking about you. When you find out what happened, you're going to go on a rampage."

I glare at the asshole. Why does he have to be so astute? "Fuck you."

Both he and Alessio laugh, "Who'd have thought that Dante 'Ice' Bianchi is being led by a woman. One that he's not yet fucked."

My hands tighten around the steering wheel.

"I wonder what it'll be like to fuck her. Will she fight? Or lay there and take it like a good girl?" Romero laughs.

I slant him a look, one that has him shutting the fuck up. My knuckles are white from the grip I have on the wheel. "One more word about my fiancée and I'll gut you where you sit."

"Fuck," Alessio whispers.

Yeah, I'm deadly serious about gutting my brother, we've all made threats before but never meant it. Until now.

"Makenna is mine."

Romero grins but keeps his damn mouth shut. Both he and Alessio have knowing smiles on their faces and if they continue, I'm going to wipe it off their faces.

"We've got your back bro," Alessio says after a couple of minutes. "We won't let dad get to her."

Damn fucking straight we won't. I know what that asshole is capable of.

"Where are we going?" Romero asks.

I grin, "I've a Russian to find." My mind is filled with the images of the bruise on Makenna's creamy skin. Some bastard put hands on her and for that he's going to pay.

THREE

Makenna

"MAKENNA..." The gentleness of my mother's voice has the hair on the back of my neck standing up. She's being nice, that can only mean she wants something.

"What, Ma?" I'm tired of this bullshit, the sooner I'm away from her the sooner I'll be able to relax. I glance in the mirror and look back at myself. The scar on my neck shining like a beacon against my tanned skin and white robe; it's a reminder that I'm nothing more than a victim in this world of monsters.

"You won't…" She stops and I turn to face her, she's sitting on the sofa, "You won't tell anyone, will you?"

I let out a bitter laugh. "Don't worry, Ma, your secret is safe with me. I'm not stupid. If I tell them what happened, what do you think is going to happen?"

She glances down at her hands, wringing them together.

"It'll mean war. Something I don't want, nor does Da, hence why this farce of a marriage is happening."

She sighs, her body slumping forward with relief, but she frowns, "You don't like your fiancé?"

I shrug, "I don't know him to make that assessment."

She lets out a little laugh and it grates on me. "You're so clinical. You've been around your uncle too long."

I take a step toward her, her eyes flash with fear before she masks it. "Why do you think that is, Ma? Hmm? If this comes out, what do you think is going to happen to you?"

She folds her arms over her chest and leans back against the sofa. "I'm married to your father, Makenna, you know just as well as I do that the Irish Mafia don't harm women."

I roll my eyes, she's fucking naïve. "You really believe that if Da finds out what happened, he'll let you live? That if Killian finds out he will?"

She gasps, "Makenna, you can't tell them."

A knock at the door gives her the reprieve she needs. "Get out, Ma, and leave me the hell alone. Today I'm getting married and then I don't want to fucking see you again."

"Watch your language, Makenna, I'm still your mother."

"You gave that right up, you're my mother in blood only…" I shake my head, she's a fucking bitch. "Get out. I have to get ready."

She huffs but does as she's told. She opens the door and finds Kinsley standing on the other side glaring at her, her silver purple bridesmaid dress hugging her curves in all the right places. She looks gorgeous. Once mom's gone, Kinsley closes the door and locks it. "What the hell did she want?"

I sit down and grab the champagne glass that's on the table. "She wanted to make sure I'd keep my mouth shut."

Kinsley's eyes flash, she's the only person that knows what happened and I trust her more than I trust anyone in this world. Kinsley will take my secret to the grave, just as I will hers. "She's a bitch, Kenna. I wish you'd change your mind and tell your dad what happened."

I raise my brow, "Take your own advice and tell Ace."

She shakes her head, her long brown hair cascading down her back. "I can't, you know that."

I nod, "I do, and you know I can't tell my da, it'll cause a fucking war."

She looks at me and I see the sorrow deep in her eyes. It's the worst thing about her knowing what happened, the look in her eyes whenever she thinks about it. I feel like I'm twelve and lying in a pool of my own blood, again.

"Shall we get you dressed?" Her voice is soft but full of support. I take another sip of champagne and get to my feet. My hair and makeup are done, all that's left is to put on my dress. "Your dress is beautiful, Kenna; you're going to look stunning."

I give her a smile, beauty is something I don't consider, not with the scar that I have. Growing up, boys would always say I was pretty, shame about the scar. Girls would make fun of it; laugh and point. I got a thick skin fast, but the shit they said, it stuck. The words Makenna and beauty don't belong in the same sentence.

She helps me get into my dress, it's tight fitting but as soon as I tried it on, I knew it was the one for me. It's got lace covering my neck so it hides my scar, it's backless and sleeveless. It hugs my hips and flows down to the ground. Beauty isn't me, but this is as close as I'll ever get. I don't think I've ever felt as sexy as I do right now wearing this dress.

Kinsley lets out a low whistle. "Damn, Kenna, Dante is going to lose his damn mind when he sees you."

At the mention of Dante my heart beats faster, there's something about that man that makes my knees go weak. I've never been one to swoon over a guy, until Dante. Whenever he touches me, my body trembles in ways that it shouldn't. I should be afraid of him. I've heard the stories about the Famiglia *made men* and the way they treat their wives and daughters, and yet whenever I look into Dante's eyes, I find a sense of peace I haven't had in a long time. To me, that's the ultimate danger. I learned that trust isn't something I should give, with the exception of Kinsley, I don't even trust my brothers. To them, the family comes first and I'll always be second. I understand that, I've known that my entire life. It's our way of life and that's the reason I can't trust them. I know if they ever knew that, they'd be hurt.

"Kenna?" Kinsley asks softly, pulling me from my thoughts. "Are you okay?"

"Yes," I reply, not sure what else I can say. I'm marrying a man I know very little about, his father is someone I hate, and I'm leaving my family behind to live with said husband.

She pulls me into her arms and I go willingly, "Promise me that you'll still come visit. That we'll still be the same. Promise me." She chokes on her words.

"Oh, Kins, of course I will. Me and you, we're not changing." If Dante thinks he can forbid me from seeing her, he's sorely mistaken.

She gasps for air and I lead her to the sofa; I should have realized she was worried. For Kinsley and I, we're practically sisters. Even when I went to live with Killian, Kinsley was there, always at my side. Hell she even came to Ireland to stay with me during the summers. If Dante doesn't allow Kinsley and I to be friends, I'll run away. For Kinsley, it would be her worst nightmare. For me, it would be the ultimate heartbreak, I'd be giving up everything I love, for her.

"It's going to be okay, Kinsley."

BLOODY UNION

She shakes her head unable to breathe. Shit.

There's a knock at the door and I quickly open it knowing I need to help Kins. I see Finn standing there with a huge smile on his face. "Finn," I whisper and his smile drops, he peers past me to see Kinsley in the midst of a panic attack. "I need your help."

He looks at me, his eyes soft. "What do you need?"

I take a deep breath, "I need you to get Dante to come here." He opens his mouth to protest but I stop him. "Please, Finn."

He nods once and turns, I close the door and go back to Kinsley; her face is red and her eyes glassy as she tries to suck in air but she's panicking too much.

I kneel down beside her, pulling her head to mine so that our foreheads are touching. "Kins, please," I say softly, hoping that she'll hear me. I need to try and get through to her. "You're meant to be the strong one. You're the one that keeps us together remember?" I bite my lip hoping to stop the onslaught of tears that's threatening to spill over. "Kinsley, you are the strongest woman I know. You are my sister."

"I'm…" she sucks in a deep breath, "scared."

I nod, my thumbs caressing her cheeks. "I know, but don't be."

"I—can't—lose—you."

I close my eyes, the pain I feel right now is unlike anything I've ever experienced. "Kins, you're not going to lose me."

"I—almost—did—once—can't—do—it—again…"

My hands on her face tighten. "You won't."

"You—almost—died—they—nearly—killed—you."
Her breathing is hard, every breath she takes sounds painful.

"Kinsley, I survived that shit. We're here. Together, we've overcome so fucking much. We're fine."

"You—don't—know—that. He—may—forbid—us—seeing—each—other."

I let out a small laugh, "You make us sound like lovers."

"You're—my—sister—Kenna—my—protector. I—need—you—please—don't—go. Please—don't—let—him—break—us." She's crying now, and it's adding to the panic.

I suck in a sharp breath, what am I supposed to say to that? She's right, if we're not allowed to be there for each other, it will break us.

"I won't." A deep voice breaks through mine and Kinsley's moment. I turn and see Dante, Romero, Alessio, and Finn standing in the room. All of their eyes on us, Dante's on me, his expression hard. Romero and Alessio's gazes bounce between Kinsley and me, whereas Finn is having a hard time keeping his emotions in check.

"You won't?" I ask in disbelief as I stand and position myself in front of Kinsley.

He stalks toward me, "I won't keep you and Kinsley away from each other. When you're at the clubhouse, you'll have three guards."

I hear Kinsley slowly start to regain her composure, her breathing doesn't sound as painful as it had.

I step closer to Dante, we're almost touching. "Just like that?"

His eyes scan my face, almost if he's searching for something. "Not just like that. Today we marry, then tomorrow, you and I talk."

I bite my lip, I should have known that he'd have stipulations.

He lowers his head, our lips almost touching. "You're

going to tell me what happened, Makenna. I can't help you if you don't." His voice is gentler than I've heard before but it still has a bite to it.

"No one can help me," I confess and watch as his eyes darken. "But, thank you anyway," I say and his features soften.

Kinsley gasps and I turn to face her, Dante's hand goes to my waist and goosebumps break out over my body. "You're not supposed to see her in her dress before the wedding."

I laugh, "Kins."

She shakes her head. "Kenna," her lips twitching, "it's bad luck."

I roll my eyes, "That's our middle name."

She laughs and to my utter surprise, walks over to Dante and hugs him. It's awkward as he's got his arm on my waist but that doesn't bother Kinsley. "Take care of her." I hear her whisper and Dante's hand on my waist tightens.

Finn clears his throat, "Hate to break this up, but everyone's waiting on us."

Kinsley pulls away from us and gives me a smile. "You ready for this?"

I shrug, "Sure, as long as there's vodka, I'm good."

She laughs and I'm glad, it's better than hearing her cry. "Why is it that Irish people drink as much as they want and it's normal?"

I smirk as I move out of Dante's hold, "You mean, when you do it, you're labelled an alcoholic?" She narrows her eyes, "It's because we can handle our liquor. You, well Kins, you get on top of a bar and start stripping."

I hear Finn's chuckle and I turn to see him. "That was once!" She gasps in mock outrage, "Better than stealing a cop car and spending the night in jail."

It's my turn to laugh, "You spent the night in jail with me, or did you forget?"

Pain slashes through her face and I feel like an ass. She quickly recovers and snorts, "Hardly. Besides, it was a good night." She slaps my ass and I narrow my eyes at her. "Your tramp stamp is something I'll never forget."

"It's not a tramp stamp when it's on my ass, Kins."

"Who the fuck tattooed your ass?"

"What the fuck?"

Dante and Finn say in unison.

Kinsley laughs and I glare at her. "Fuck, will you both calm the hell down."

"No, I want to know what fucking asshole put his hands on you and tattooed your ass," Finn demands and Kinsley's eyes widen, he's not as aggressive around Kinsley as he is now.

"Why?"

"Because I'm going to kill him," Dante snarls.

I can't contain the burst of laughter that escapes me.

"Makenna, this isn't funny," Finn growls.

"What's not funny?" Da asks as he strolls into the room, Patrick and Cian hot on his heels.

"Makenna let some asshole tattoo her ass."

"What the fuck?" Patrick snaps and I resist the urge to roll my eyes.

"Shit," Kinsley whispers.

"You all need to calm the hell down." I tell them glaring at them all, Da however is standing in the doorway with a smile on his face.

"Tell us, Kenna," Cian pleads with me.

"Makenna's right, you all need to calm down. What the hell did I raise? A pack of wild animals?"

Finn turns his gaze to our father, his features cool and calm but I can see him internally battling with his anger.

"Christ. It was Kinsley," Da tells them. "You know what those two are fucking like when they've been on the tear. They do stupid shit, hell getting a tattoo wasn't even the worst shit they did that night. They thought it would be funny to get a tattoo and I told them both that they weren't allowed to have anyone tattoo them. So they decided it would be funnier if they tattooed each other. So Kinsley gave Kenna a tatt and Kenna gave Kinsley one. Now do you want to calm the fuck down and relax? Today is supposed to be a joyous occasion, we finally managed to get someone to marry your sister."

"Hey!" I cry out. "I'm a fucking catch!" Da grins and my brothers laugh. "It's these fucking idiots you have to worry about. None of them know how to keep their cocks in their pants. No woman is going to want to marry their crotch infested asses."

"Leave me the hell out of this. I did nothing wrong!" Cian says holding up his hands.

"Oh, I'm sorry," I say sarcastically. "I forgot who it was that I walked in on while they were fucking two whores."

"You should have knocked." He growls.

"It was in the fucking pool at seven in the damn morning!"

Da smacks him around the head, "What did I tell you about those fucking whores?"

"Okay, it's time for you all to leave. Makenna needs to finish getting ready and Dante needs to be at the altar waiting for her."

Everyone except Dante leaves and I turn to him, butterflies swarm in my stomach as I wait for him to say what he wants. He turns to Kinsley, "Can you give us a minute?"

She bites her lip and gives him a tight nod, before turning to leave.

"Are you okay?" he asks closing the distance between us.

I look at him in shock, he's showing concern for me, that's something I didn't think he'd do, ever. "I'm okay," I tell him gently and I'm rewarded as he gives me a stunningly soft smile.

He's so close, I could reach out and touch him, I'm itching to do it. His eyes soften as he looks at me. "That was fucking intense, Makenna."

I do what I've been itching to do and place my hand on his chest, his heart beat is slow and steady and it settles me. "Kenna, my family call me Kenna."

He searches my face and nods. "Kenna." It rolls off his tongue and I let it wash over me. Loving how he says it. "It was intense, she's your girl, are you okay?"

I bite my lip to stop my tears from falling, I feel his strong heartbeat and let it settle me again. "I'm okay, she's not been like that in a while and seeing her like that hurt. But I'm okay, and thanks to you, she's going to be."

He's quiet for a moment, "I meant what I said, tomorrow, we're talking."

I nod, "I know and I think I knew this day would come. Not tonight though, Dante, let's just enjoy today and then tomorrow, we'll deal with the ugly stuff."

His head lowers so that our lips are barely touching, "You're ugly stuff is going to be mine, the sooner you realize that I'm going to protect you from anything and everything that poses any harm to you, the better we'll both be."

"I know you want to help, but it's going to take a while to trust you." His eyes narrow at my words and for some reason I want to ease his worries, "I don't trust many people, including my brothers, so please don't be offended."

I've shocked him, but he quickly recovers and in doing so, he lowers his mouth to mine and gives me a quick, hard kiss.

"Fuck," I mutter when he leans back.

"I'll see you in a bit," he says as he walks to the door. My heart is pounding and yet he seems completely unfazed. "And Kenna…" he calls as he opens the door. "You look beautiful."

My heart melts at his words.

This isn't good. This marriage was supposed to be an arrangement, I wasn't supposed to get attached, to catch feelings. Knowing that the made men of the Famiglia are cruel, it would only hurt more when they abuse me. But Dante, he's given me hope and that's one thing that can break me.

FOUR

Makenna

"YOU REALLY DO LOOK BEAUTIFUL, MAKENNA," Kinsley tells me as she dabs her eyes.

My stomach is full of butterflies fluttering their wings frantically against my belly. My nerves have kicked in but for some reason I'm not scared. When I was told that I'd be marrying Dante, every scenario went through my mind. I always pictured being scared, being so distraught that I'd be a shivering mess. Instead, I'm calm and ready. Everything I've come to know about Dante is that he's a monster, but not to me. The soft look he gives me makes my body react in ways I can't explain. Thinking about this day, I thought I'd be in hell, but I'm looking forward to our future. Although, I'm not sure how it will go but I'm hopeful and that's a good thing.

"What do you think of Dante?" I ask her, smoothing down my dress.

Her eyes widen, "Um…"

I laugh, "Kins, you're my best friend. You know how to read people, you've been doing it since you were a child. What do you think of Dante?"

She sighs and takes a seat on the sofa, "Makenna, that man doesn't know how to love..." hearing her say those words is like a punch in the gut. "From the little I've seen you interact, he's not a maniac around you, the two of you could have a reasonable marriage but that's about it."

I close my eyes and sit beside her. "Do you think he'll push me to tell him what happened?"

She nods, "Definitely. He's possessive of you already. The hand to the waist, the smouldering looks. He's going to want to know everything about you, including what happened *that* night."

"I can't tell him everything," I whisper, there's no way I can.

She reaches for my hand and gives me a reassuring squeeze. "You need to set the boundaries, Kenna. Make him be truthful, that way, there's no surprises. But if that happens, it means you have to be completely honest too."

"Grr." I cry, "Why do you have to be so wise?"

She laughs before sobering, "You need to decide what you want. You can keep him in the dark, but I know you, I know that if that happened, you'll be miserable. If you're honest, then make him be too."

"Let's see how tonight goes and then I'll decide." I still don't think it'll be wise telling him everything.

"Okay, but think about how it will impact your marriage if you don't be honest with him." She gives my hand one more squeeze before getting to her feet.

"Kins, he'll want to know about you too."

She nods, "Yeah, I know, I'm okay with that."

I get to my feet. "You are?" Since fucking when? "You've made me keep this shit quiet for years, Kins, years! I could have had Da sort this out, hell, I would have done it."

"It would have caused a war!" she whispers.

"And you don't think telling Dante what's going on, will cause one?"

"You won't let it."

I laugh, I can't help it, she's got an awful lot of faith in me. "I don't see how that will happen. Anyone who finds out what's happening isn't going to sit back and let it continue." I hate that it's gone on for this long already. If I had a choice, I'd have made sure it ended from the get go.

She shrugs, "When my father dies, then I'll be free."

I shake my head. "Your dad is a piece of shit, Kins; he's letting you get hurt and doesn't give a shit."

"I think that Stuart has something on him, that's why he's letting him do it."

My anger is bubbling beneath the surface, we've spoken at length about this in the past and this is the first time that she's telling me this. "It doesn't matter if he has something on him. You don't let your daughter be hurt! You just don't fucking do it."

"I think my father killed my grandfather."

I suck in a sharp breath, Kinsley and I aren't supposed to have secrets, but we do. We've both hidden things from one another in the past, this is one of them. "What makes you think that?"

She glances down at her hands and then back to me, "He was a bastard, Kenna. He really was, was worse than dad. He lashed out on Ace more than anyone, but then Ace got bigger and then he turned his attention on me."

I know what happened, Ace came to me, hoping that I'd help him by asking my father for a favor. Ace believes that my da will call him when he needs a marker.

"What happened to him?" I never want anyone to know that I was the one that poisoned the bastards coke stash. If it comes out, then there will be war. The secrets I carry are there to stop the people I love from getting hurt.

She shrugs, "The cocaine he had was shit." She shakes her head, a small smile playing on her lips. "He wasn't found until morning."

"Why are we even talking about this? The man's been dead for almost six years, why bring it up?"

She bites her lip, she's thinking carefully about what she says. Everyone sees her and sees this gorgeous brunette who is just the princess of the Vipers Fury Motorcycle club, but she's manipulative when she needs to be and that's most of the damn time. "Don't." I warn her, she's never like this with me and I'm pissed off that she's starting now. "Kins, whatever the hell you have to say, say it."

"Fine," she breathes, "we're talking about this because I need to know what happened, Kenna. I need to know why the hell my father is letting that animal hurt me whenever he likes."

"I don't know, Kins. I really wish I knew why this was happening. I've tried so hard to take you away from them but you never would leave. You kept going back." I would have kept her with me at all times, every time she went back made me lose a part of myself. How can I protect my best friend if she willingly went back into that hell? Instead, every time it happened, I'd get a phone call and I'd have to be the one to get her. Bring her home with me and stitch up her wounds, clean up her cuts, and hold her while she cried until she fell asleep.

"I had to go back. If I didn't, they'd have come for me. You and I both know that. We're the same Kenna, we both do whatever the hell we have to, ensuring the ones we love are safe. So I go home and I take what that asshole does and then I call the only person in this world that I can rely on. The girl that's been my best friend since as long as I can remember. The one who's had my back from the very first moment we met and the woman who's been my backbone."

I will the tears not to fall, "Don't make me cry!" I warn her. "You've been here for me just as much as I've been there for you. You also cleaned up all the cuts and bruises I've had."

She nods, "Let's hope I'm right about your soon to be husband. I don't want to clean up any more cuts."

I reach for her and pull her into my arms, "I don't want to clean anymore of yours, but until your father dies, I'm going to have to." I release her and take a step back, once again, smoothing down my dress. "It's time."

She reaches for the bouquet and hands it to me. "Try not to kill my father as you walk past him."

I grin, "Your dad's here? Who the hell invited him?"

She shakes her head, gone is all the seriousness and in its place is happiness, just the way it should be today. "Let's get you married."

I exit the door and I'm greeted by my father, "Have you two been behaving?"

"Don't we always?"

His brows practically hit his forehead. "Now, the day you two start acting like ladies, is the day, I begin to worry."

"You love us really, Mr Gallagher." Kinsley grins.

Dad shakes his head, "Kinsley, how many times have I told you to call me Seamus?"

She ignores him and turns to me, "I'll leave you both alone for a few moments."

Dad waits until she's out of sight before turning to me. "Baby girl."

I shake my head, "Don't, Da…" It's been a long time since I was this emotional. Today, my life is changing and I'm not sure if it's for better or worse.

"No, I've failed you."

"You haven't," I implore, needing him to realize he did what he needed to do.

"Kenna, will you be quiet for a minute so I can talk?" I nod. "Thank you, as I was saying. I've failed you. I couldn't keep you safe even though that was my job. You're my baby, Kenna, and I've fucked up in more ways than one. I'm sorry."

"Da, you've done what you thought was right. This is our way of life, this marriage is what we do. It's going to bring peace between the Italians and the Irish. Besides, I could marry worse than Dante."

Da scoffs, "Yeah, if you say so. The boy's a fucking psycho. He's not what you think, he's everyone's worst nightmare."

I laugh, "And, I'm the one that gets to marry him."

"Remember, you're a Gallagher Kenna, through and through. Even after you take the Italian bastard's name, you're still ours, and we'll always protect you." There's a promise in his words, he's letting me know that no matter what, he's going to be there for me.

"I'll be fine," I promise him.

He kisses my cheek, "I know you will be. I'm proud of you."

My heart swells at his words. "Da, you've got to stop, otherwise I'm going to cry."

He shakes his head, "My Kenna doesn't cry."

"You don't know me, Da, not anymore." His eyes flash with guilt and I feel bad, "Sorry, I didn't mean it like that."

"You did," he says simply. "I sent you away hoping to protect you."

I know he did, if only he knew the life he had sent me away to.

"You hate me for it, don't you?"

"Da, I don't hate you..." not anymore. "You did what you thought was right. That's all that I can ever ask of you." I place a kiss on his cheek, "I don't hate you, Da, I don't. So, we're going to put a smile on our faces and I'm going to get married. Besides, I'll be back on Sunday."

He smiles, "Yeah, you will. You're not allowed to miss Sunday dinner unless you're dying. That includes that husband of yours."

I lift my brows, "Dante doesn't seem to go anywhere without his brothers."

Dad's eyes narrow, "Fuck, do I really have to sit around a table with those Italian bastards?"

"Da!" I gasp, "you've got to stop calling them bastards."

He laughs and I can't help but smile. "Let's get you married, huh?"

He holds out his arm for me to take and I do. A few sharp turns from my dressing room and we come to the doors of church. "I love you, Da," I whisper as the bridal march song starts.

"And I love you, Makenna."

The door opens and my breath is taken from me when I see Dante standing at the front of the altar, his eyes on me.

Kinsley walks ahead, I notice that Romero's eyes follow her every move, her body tenses ever so slightly as she passes her father and brother on her way to the altar.

My arm tightens on Dad's as we move toward Dante and the priest. My mother has outdone herself today. The church is full to the brim, the who's who of the Mafia world are here and then some. The men of the East Street Kings are here, Landon, Scantor, Miller, and Prior. In front of them is Hudson Brady, along with his wife Mia, and his right hand man, Jagger, and his wife, Sarah. Dante's family take up a huge portion of the church, each and every single one of them are armed to the teeth.

I finally make it to Dante and once again, my breath is taken from me; his gaze is piercing me as he stares at me. He shakes Da's hand and the priest begins to talk, but I'm unable to concentrate on what he's saying. Dante has a hard grasp on my hand, his thumb rubbing circles against my palm. I'm in a daze, I can't help but glance up at him throughout the ceremony, and whenever I do, he always seems to catch me.

When the priest says, "You may now kiss the bride." My heart speeds up and I glance at Dante once more. His eyes are filled with lust and need as he lowers his lips down on mine, gently and yet promising. It's a promise of what's yet to come. I cling onto him as though he's my lifeline and I'm wondering when the hell I became this woman? The woman that wants someone in their life, to be a part of it, in ways that no one else has?

"Dante…" I whisper and his gaze hits my lips.

"Kenna…" he replies and I practically whimper.

The sound of glass shattering breaks through our moment and I cry out as something hits my arm. I'd have fallen to the ground if Dante had not been holding onto me. His eyes narrow in on my arm and I'm too scared to see what's wrong; what's made that dark look come onto his face?

Then all hell breaks loose as the doors burst open, showing the Bratva holding guns. Dante pushes me behind him as he pulls out his own gun.

Shit, this is going to be a bloody wedding.

FIVE

Dante

MY HEART BATTERS against my chest as I watch Makenna walk down the aisle, there's something about this woman that fucking gets to me and I don't even know her. When my father told me that I'd be marrying, I had assumed that the relationship I'd have with my wife would be cold and sterile. I know the way things work in our world, women are to be seen and not heard. They're to make a home and look after the children, but as I watch Makenna walk toward me there's no way things will be cold or sterile. The woman makes my blood run hot, she's brought out a protective instinct I never knew I had. When Finn told me that Makenna wanted me, I didn't know what to expect but walking into the room and watching her kneel in front of a panicked Kinsley wasn't it. Hearing them talk made me realize that I've underestimated my soon-to-be wife. Her words hit me like a fucking sledgehammer, *"I survived that shit. We're here. Together, we've overcome so fucking much. We're fine."*

She's far from fucking fine, seeing the two women huddled together, heads touching, made me see that there're things Makenna hasn't let anyone see. I'm determined to find out what the hell she's been through and I'm not going to stop until I find out all of her secrets. I'm unable to take my eyes off her, she has a bright smile on her face. You'd think we've known each other for years the way her smile lights the room. Whereas the truth is so much worse, she's been handed to me in a fucking deal, and yet she's not showing an ounce of fear. She's strong and vulnerable. She's a walking, talking contradiction and yet I crave her.

I shake Seamus' hand and instantly grasp Makenna's, my thumb moving in circles over her skin, needing this contact. Goosebumps break out over her skin and I bite back a smirk; she's affected by me. When my lips touch hers, it takes all my restraint not to take it further. Instead I pull back, my hands on her hips, holding her tight. Her eyes are heavy with lust. She's fucking gorgeous, she's holding onto me as though she needs the strength to keep her upright.

"Dante…" she whispers and my cock stirs, my gaze goes to her lips, plump and kissable.

"Kenna…." I reply gruffly, pissed that we're in a church and not near a bed.

Glass shatters and she jerks in my arms just as a cry escapes her, I reach for my gun as the doors to the church burst open.

The fucking Bratva.

The blood on Kenna's arm has my blood pumping, murder running through my veins. They fucking shot her. They're going to pay for it. Tightening my grip on her waist, I twist her so that she's behind me, my gun in hand and I start shooting.

"Shit," Romero says and I glance at him, his eyes on Alessio, who's on the floor bleeding.

BLOODY UNION

Kenna pulls out of my hold and I hear material ripping, more shots are being fired and I focus on the bastards shooting at my wife and brothers. As far as I can tell there's thirty, if not more, Russian bastards here. They picked the wrong fucking wedding to hit. Every man here is firing back at them, we're taking them down but they just keep coming.

"We need to get him out of here." Kenna's voice pulls me through the blood lust I have. "Dante, if we don't he's going to die."

Fuck.

"Finn!" she yells and instantly her brother's by our side. "I need you to cover us, we need to get Alessio out of here."

He instantly nods, crooking his finger, his men are surrounding us.

"We need to go out the back, there's a car waiting."

I turn back to my wife and I'm fucking shocked, she's torn off the bottom half of her wedding dress. Blood covers her torso, and I'm not sure if it's hers or my brothers, seeing as the bottom half of her dress is on Alessio's body where Kinsley is applying pressure. But what shocks me the most is her calm like appearance, her mind clear as she barks orders at people.

"Romero, I need you to carry Alessio out. Kins, Ace is waiting for you."

"Keep a tight perimeter. Shoot anyone who gets close," Finn tells his men and they instantly nod. "Let's go."

"Dante," Kenna whispers and for the first time, I hear a tremor of fear in her voice. "If you have to stay, I understand."

Fuck, this woman. She understands. I don't even have to say a word and she knows what I need. For the second time today, her hand lays over my heart and she takes a deep breath. "Be safe," she whispers and places a kiss against my lips before she releases me and they leave.

I turn back to the foray and see that most of the attendees have left, leaving my men, the Irish and a few others left, there's still some Bratva left but nowhere as near as many as there was. I walk toward my men, "I want at least one alive." I want to find out just why they started shooting up my wedding.

"How's Makenna?" Seamus asks and it's in that moment that I realize, I didn't even check. I knew she'd been shot, but I don't know how bad. Fuck. He shakes his head.

"Finn's with her, they're making their escape."

He nods, "Let's get rid of the rest of these bastards and then you can go and check yeah?" There's a fucking threat in there somewhere, there always seems to be with Seamus, he can't just come out and say whatever the fuck he wants instead the asshole has to say some cryptic shit.

"Boss," I hear one of my men call and I turn to face Stefan. He's got a cut to his eyebrow, a bruise forming on his cheek and he's grinning like a crazy asshole.

"What?"

"Boss, the Russian's have retreated, there were four Escalades coming to the entrance and then they left. We've got three in the back of the car, we're bringing them to the warehouse."

My gut tightens at his words. "I need to find my wife. Fuckers are probably following her."

Stefan's grin fades, "Boss, what do you need?"

"Get them to the warehouse. Make sure you're not followed and that they have no weapons. Once I make sure my wife is safe, I'll be there." He nods once and turns.

"Want me to help locate her?" Seamus asks.

"No, it won't take me long." I turn, not wanting to deal

with this shit any longer. She's my wife now, he has to come to terms with that. I make my way out the back just in time to see my wife shooting a fucking Russian bastard. Why the hell has she got a gun in her hands? My rage starts to surface again, she's already been hurt and now she's just killed a man. Fuck.

"Kenna." Her name is a growl from my lips.

Her back stiffens and she turns to glare at me, "You here to help?" Her Irish accent is thicker than I've heard it before.

My cock starts to stir again, her defiance shouldn't be a turn on, but it is. "Sure," I drawl and see her lips turn up before she quells her features.

"There's six out front," she tells me. "Fucking Finn told me to stay here while he took the men with him. Arsehole." She shakes her head. "Fuck knows where they've gone. Thankfully, Romero isn't stupid and had a gun."

"Where did you get that one?" I ask her and I'm surprised I'm able to keep my tone even.

She raises her brow and shakes her head. "When Romero put a bullet into arsehole number one," she points to the dead body on the floor beside her, "I picked his gun up and used it on arsehole number two and three. Now, I've answered your question and as you can see I'm not going to have a meltdown because I killed someone; wasn't the first time and certainly won't be the last. How about we cut the chit chat and get to the car before your brother bleeds to death?"

I bite back my chuckle, whereas Romero and Alessio don't. Fuck, I should hate that she's not the quiet, shy woman I had expected but I'm not, I'm glad. I don't want a docile wife, I want someone who's full of life and looking at Kenna that's what I've got. "Let's go."

"Atta boy." Kenna laughs and I shake my head, fuck,

how can I want to laugh during a moment like this? "The black Rolls, that's where we're heading. Try not to get shot," she tells me.

"Don't worry, princess, I'll be fine."

She smirks at me, "Good, you have your husband duties to take care of tonight."

Jesus! My cock twitches at the thought of being inside of her. "Oh, princess, nothing, and I mean nothing will stop me from fucking you tonight."

Her pupils dilate, then she shakes her head and runs out the back door, firing her gun as she does.

"I'm going to kill her," I grunt as I follow behind her.

She's standing in the middle of the parking lot shooting at the bastards. I snap out of my shock and start shooting too. There's only a couple more of the fuckers left, and within seconds there's more gunfire, the Irish are coming out of the front and taking them down. "Kenna, into the car now," I shout at her and thankfully she has more sense than to argue with me. She runs to the car, fucking runs in her six inch heels like she's been doing it every day of her life, and opens the doors. She pulls the back door open and jumps into the driver's side.

Romero's right behind me, pulling Alessio along with him. I reach for Alessio and Romero runs around the other side of the car. Looking down at my youngest brother, I see the pale skin and the sheen of sweat on his head, he's not doing good. FUCK! Romero gets in and helps me put Alessio onto the back seat. Within seconds I'm around the car and sliding into the passenger's side. Makenna doesn't wait for me to put my seatbelt on, she puts the car into drive and pulls out of the parking lot.

When we put some distance between us and the church, my pulse starts to slow down, though the anger I have is still palpable. The fuckers shot my brother and wife.

I'm going to kill every single one of them as soon as we get them safe.

"Phone, please?" Kenna asks not looking at me and I frown but hand it to her. "Thanks," she whispers and gives me a small smile as she punches in some numbers.

Ringing filters through the silent car and I realize she must have put it onto speaker. "Hello?" A man answers.

"Doc, it's Makenna."

"Ah, my dear, congratulations are in order so I hear."

"Thanks, Doc. We ran into a bit of trouble," she tells him; not once has she taken her eyes off the road.

"Say no more. Same place?" he asks and my body tightens.

"Yep, I'll be there before you." Her face is blank, not a single emotion is running through her head.

"Okay, dear, I'll be there shortly."

She ends the call and I'm surprised to see her once again punching in numbers; the car's filled with the sound of ringing. "Hello?" This time it's a woman that answers.

"Angela, I'll be there in fifteen minutes. Get the guest rooms set up, the doc's on his way. I'm going to need the usual shit."

"Of course, Ms Gallagher."

"Bianchi," she replies instantly and I smile. Damn, she surprises me at every turn.

"Of course, I'm sorry. I'll get right on it, Mrs Bianchi. And congratulations, darling." She once again ends the call and this time she passes me my cell.

"Where are we going?" Romero asks.

"My place. This is off the grid, nobody, other than Angela and the doc knows where it is. Kinsley has been inside but she doesn't know where it is. Keep the pressure on his wound," she instructs him.

"Why?" I ask, why would she need a house off the grid?

"Why, what?" She says with a frown.

"Why does nobody know where it is?"

She shrugs, "Because I didn't want them to know. I prefer having somewhere I know is clean and that if I need to I can go."

"So many secrets, Makenna." My voice is low but there's a bite to it.

She laughs, "Oh, Dante, you have no idea who the hell you've married. I've so many fucking secrets I'm drowning in them."

Everyone's silent as we weave through the city, heading toward the suburbs. I'm wondering where the hell she's leading us, when she comes to a stop at an iron gate; trees surround it so you can't see anything. From outside it looks as though it's an abandoned lot, but when Makenna drives through the gates, I realize it's a fucking mansion. The building is at least five stories high, huge windows cover the majority of the downstairs as well as scattered around the upper floors. There's an obnoxious sculpture of a cherub on the lawn. Everything about this place screams money. It doesn't fit with what I have seen of Makenna so far. She's not flashy like her father.

The garage door opens and she drives into it. Before anyone can react, she's turning off the car and sliding out. I'm a nanosecond behind her, rushing to her side and opening the door to get Alessio out. "Let's go, we need to get the bullet out and stop the bleeding."

She leads us to an elevator, where she punches in a code. The doors slide open and she waves for us to go ahead. The doors close and she hits the button, the elevator purrs as it starts to ascend. "Holy shit, this is like some James Bond type shit." Romero breathes and I want to rip his fucking head off for the look he's giving my wife.

"Angela?" Makenna yells as soon as we're out of the elevator.

"Mrs Bianchi…" A woman in her late fifties appears, wiping her hands on a cloth that's attached to her apron. "I have the room set up, please let me know if you need anything."

The two women start walking and I'm getting fucking annoyed; I hate being in the dark. Finally we reach a door and Makenna opens it. "Put him on the bed," she instructs gently as her eyes survey the room and the instruments at the side of the bed. "Angela, the doc will be arriving soon, please let him in when he gets here."

"Of course, Mrs Bianchi."

"Shit," Makenna groans as she rubs her head. "Angela this is my husband, Dante, and his brothers, Romero and Alessio."

"Mr Bianchi." She grins at me and shakes my hand, taking my attention away from my wife and to the woman shaking my hand as though she's just met the damn pope. "It's a pleasure to meet you. Can I get you anything? Coffee, beer, whiskey?"

"Whiskey neat, please, Ma'am."

She nods, "Certainly sir." She turns on her heel and leaves the room.

"Dante, take your belt off please." Makenna asks and I see her looking over Alessio. She's taken off his jacket and ripped open his shirt, blood pooling from his wound. He's lost a lot of blood; too much blood.

I frown but do as she asks. As soon as I hand it to her, she folds it in half and turns her attention back to Alessio. "I'm really sorry, but this is going to hurt. I'm going to need you to bite down on this." As soon as he does, she goes silent, putting on a pair of disposable gloves and picks up tweezers. "He's going to end up passing out. There's no other way, I don't have anything to give him for the pain." She looks at me and I see the depth of despair in her eyes, she's worried about hurting him. Does she think that I'll punish her for doing so? I nod, unable to say anything.

I watch in sick fascination as she gets to work, pulling the bullet out of him; Alessio grunts around the belt, his eyes full of pain. Romero slides up beside me, he too hasn't been able to take his eyes off the scene in front of him. "Angela?" Makenna yells and instantly the lady is rushing into the room, two glasses of Whiskey in her hands and passes them to Romero and I.

"Yes, Mrs Bianchi?"

"Jesus, Angela, how long have you known me?" Her tone isn't impatient, instead full of love.

"Since you were six."

Makenna nods, "And yet you still won't call me Makenna."

Angela shakes her head, "Oh no, I can't do that."

Makenna grimaces before sighing. "Fine. Will you please call the doc and see what's taking him so damn long?" She glances at me, "What blood type is Alessio?"

I stare at her in confusion, how the fuck am I supposed to know that shit?

"Angela, find out his blood type and inform the doc, he's going to need a transfusion."

"Of course, I'll do that right away. Do you need anything else?"

"No, thank you. I'm okay. I'm almost done here, I just need doc and the blood."

Angela nods and runs out of the room. "I just have to stitch him up, thankfully, it didn't hit anything major. He's lost a lot of blood but he'll be fine as long as it doesn't get infected. Once the doctor gets here, he'll give him the antibiotics and transfusion."

"Jesus, how the hell do you know how to do this shit?" Romero asks as she begins to put stitches in Alessio.

"Practice, years and years of practice," she murmurs, her attention fully on what she's doing.

I'm wondering even more what secrets she holds; this woman is a mystery, one I intend on solving.

Hearing my phone ring, I reach into my pocket, pull the phone out and quickly answer. "Yeah?" I bark, not in the mood for pleasantries.

"Boss," It's Stefan. "We've got a fucking problem. Those assholes we brought back to the warehouse, well they're dead."

"How the fuck are they dead?" I clip. What the fuck is wrong with these motherfuckers? They had one job. Just one and they can't even do that right.

"Fucker's must have had it planned. We were ambushed, fuckers shot up our vehicle. But they managed to hit the three bastards in the back and not Marco or I."

Fucking Bratva. How the fuck are they one step ahead?

"I'll check in tomorrow. I want every man on this. I want to find the bastards who shot up my wedding and then shot the prisoners we had."

"On it, Boss."

I end the call and look back at Makenna. Today has been a fucking clusterfuck. My wife has too many fucking secrets, but I'm going to find out every single one of them.

SIX

Makenna

I STARE DOWN at my hands, Alessio's blood coats them, even with the disposable gloves on. Alessio passed out once I removed the bullet. For the first time in my life, I was worried. Usually I've only had to stitch myself or Kinsley up. But today I had to do it to Alessio, my new brother-in-law, knowing that there was two people watching as I did; two men that wouldn't hesitate to put a bullet in my head if I messed up. I was worried that if I did mess up, what would happen? I hate this unnerving feeling I have. It's not me. I don't care what people think, I never have.

Growing up with older brothers it helps shape you, they take you under their wing and teach you to take care of yourself. Show you how to be strong and resilient, show you what it's like to not be afraid and I wasn't. Until that day. The day when the facade fell and I came face to face with the devil incarnate. Then the young girl that was fun and outgoing became the woman I am today. Since then I've learned a lot of things about myself about the world and I've used every single thing to my advantage.

"Kenna?" His warm tone makes me look up from my hands.

"Mrs Bianchi…" Angela calls out just as Dante's hand grips hold of my hip. Having him so close makes me shiver. "The doc's here."

I nod, "Thank you, Angela, you may go home now."

She glances between me and Dante. "Thank you, I have dinner for you all, and the guest rooms are made up."

I give her a soft smile, one that she returns. "Send the doc up and have a good evening."

Within seconds, the doc is walking into the room, he takes a sweeping glance at us before moving to Alessio. "Nice work, Makenna, not that I should be surprised. You're an old hand at this now. Must make a change from stitching yourself up."

The hand on my hip tightens as the air in the room changes, this is more dangerous.

I ignore everyone and focus on what the doc's doing. Hanging the antibiotics, before giving him the blood transfusion. It takes a while, nobody says anything we're all watching the doc intently. Well Romero and I are, Dante however, has his gaze firmly on me. I glance up and I'm shocked by the intense gaze he has on me. My hand reaches for his and I hold it tight. Up until today, I hadn't really had anyone to lean on, but right now, in this instance I have Dante. I'm not sure how long it will last but I'll take whatever is on offer, for however long it lasts.

"Do you want me to have a look at your arm?" Doc asks and I shake my head. Up until that moment, I had forgotten that I had been shot. It's just a graze, but the pain has hit now. "I'll leave the gauze and things for you. You know the drill. I'll be by tomorrow to check on Mr Bianchi here." He packs up his bag and starts to head out.

"Thanks, Doc, I'll see you tomorrow." He nods before he leaves the room.

"Romero, would you like me to show you to your room?" At my words, Romero's gaze leaves Alessio and moves to me; the softness in his eyes is unlike I've ever seen. He gives me a sharp nod. "Follow me." I take my hand away from Dante and realize I've left blood on him. "Sorry," I whisper as I rip the gloves off me and throw them into the trash beside the bed.

He doesn't take his hand from my hip, instead his other hand goes to the other side. We're all still in our wedding attire and I'm dying to strip off and put on something more comfortable. But first, I need a goddamn shower.

We walk out of the room and I leave the door ajar, needing to hear in case Alessio needs any help. We walk down the hall, "Romero, your room is on your right. There's food in the kitchen, help yourself to anything you need."

He gives me a nod as he walks toward the bedroom door, when his hand touches the handle. "Thank you for saving him," he says softly.

"Good night, Romero," I reply, not wanting to answer any questions. I know they all have some, but there's only one person who's going to demand them and right now, I don't have it in me to answer them. Not now.

Dante and I are silent as we make our way to my room. I've not been here in a couple of weeks. This house has been my safe haven. It will always be and yet, today, I let three men I barely know walk into it. That's something that has never happened before and I'm still trying to figure out why I did this.

Once we reach my room, I close the door behind us. The floor length mirror in front of me shows me just how fucked up I look. When Alessio went down in the church and I saw the blood pouring out of him, I did the only thing I could. I reached for the skirt of my dress and I pulled as hard as I could, ignoring the ripping sound as I tore it from my body. I couldn't think about what I was doing, I just did what I had to. But staring at myself, all I see is what I am. A bloody bride. Blood covers my arms, legs, face and what's left of my dress. I look like a fucking corpse. My gaze goes to the man behind me; his focus is on me. His eyes dark and hard, as he too takes in my appearance.

"I guess I know what everyone's going to call me now," I say with a laugh. Although it's forced, it's all I can do to stop the tears.

"And what's that?" His voice is a rumble.

"Bloody bride."

"Anyone calls you that, I'll kill them." It's a promise.

I shrug, "It's what I am. Our wedding turned into a bloody union, Dante."

He spins me around and I crash against his body. "I don't give a fuck." He growls, "You're not a bloody bride. Why wouldn't you let the doctor see your arm?"

I shake my head. "I don't like anyone touching me."

I watch as his features darken, "You let me."

I'm speechless, I have no idea what to say without making myself sound like a complete bitch. "I haven't let anyone near me with a sharp object since someone slit my throat." He opens his mouth to say something but it's too much. I pull away from him and walk into the bathroom, I need to see what my arm's like. I managed to tie a piece of fabric from my dress around it after Kinsley helped me in the church with Alessio. Untying the fabric I see the bleeding has stopped, it's not as bad as I had feared. I won't need stitches but it'll leave a mark. What's one more to add to the mix? I clean the wound and leave it be, I need a shower and putting a bandage on it will be pointless at this stage.

"Kenna..." It's a gruff whisper, I shouldn't turn around and face him, but he has a pull over me, one that I can't ignore. "Fuck." He grabs hold of my waist and spins me around so that I'm facing him. "You're supposed to be this docile woman who knows her place."

I scoff, "Whoever gave you that impression needs to be shot."

His lips twitch, "How did you know how to fix Alessio? How do you drive like you're born to do it? Driving at full speed, without breaking a sweat? How the fuck do you know how to shoot a gun and hit the target every time?"

"Dante..." I whisper, we weren't supposed to be doing this tonight. "Tomorrow." Even then I doubt I'll be able to do it.

"You drive me fucking crazy. What the hell am I going to do with you?"

I laugh, "You're my husband, Dante. I'm sure you can come up with something creative..."

His hands tighten on my hips and he lifts me up. Instinctively, my legs wrap around his waist, my arms going around his neck. His lips are on mine. It's hot, hard, demanding. I sink into his embrace, his hands sliding from my hips to my ass, pulling my body against his thickening cock. I moan, grinding against it. There's something about Dante that makes me lose myself. Whenever I'm around him, I feel the heat between us. His tongue sweeps into my mouth, stealing my breath. I push back with my own. My hands fisting into his hair, pulling his head closer to mine.

It's only when my back hits the bed and he's leaning over me do I realize that he walked us from the bathroom to the bedroom. I'm in such a lust filled haze that I have no idea what's going on. "This dress needs to come off," he growls, the sound reverberating in his chest.

I lick my lips, "You don't like it?" I'm breathless.

His eyes are dark with lust, "I didn't say that. It's fucking tight, it clings to you. It shows me what's underneath and right now, I need it off, so I can see all of my bride."

I squirm beneath him, God, why do I find that a turn on? I hear the unmistakable snap, my body freezes as I see his switchblade in his hands. Is he for real? I don't fight, instead I stay still. I learned from a very young age not to show fear.

"Kenna…" His voice sounds hoarse but I ignore it. "I'm not going to hurt you."

Now where have I heard that before? Oh yeah, right before my throat got slit. I don't trust anyone, I can't afford to. Look where trust got me.

"Baby, I promise." He sounds as though he's hurting, but I'm not focusing on him, my eyes are glued on the knife in his hands.

"Do it," I demand, whatever the fuck he's doing, just do it and get it over with.

With the flick of his hand, the knife slices through my dress, the ripping sound loud through the silence of the room. As soon as he's finished cutting my dress, he folds the knife away and puts it back in his pocket. The dress falls away from my body, leaving me completely naked except for the tiny, white, lacy G-string. I've never had a problem with nudity, but laid bare before him, I feel oddly exposed in a way I've never felt. I lift my chin high, not willing to show any weakness.

"Come back to me… Kenna…. Come back." His lips are on my neck, kissing and sucking. "Baby, come back." My hands go to his hair and my back arches as his lips capture my nipple, his teeth grazing them and I gasp. "That's it."

My hands tighten in his hair and I pull. He raises a brow at me, the stupid asshole has a smirk on his face. "Next time you hold a knife against me, I'll kill you."

That smirk of his widens but his eyes flash with something dark. "Yet another question. Tell me something Makenna, why do I get the feeling that killing me would come easy to you?"

I ignore the stupid question, my hand reaching between our bodies for his zipper. I pull it down and his cock springs free. "Are you going to stare at me, or are you going to fuck me?" I breathe, needing him. He only has to touch me and my body is alight, it's as though my blood is on fire as it runs through my veins.

He sucks in a sharp breath. "I know what you're doing," he murmurs as he lifts off me. I watch as he strips down. His shirt comes off first and his muscles are tight, just as he probably is. Dante is a closed book, or so they say. He doesn't show any emotion. Yet looking at my husband, I say they're wrong, Dante's lust is an emotion and I'm wondering what other emotions I can invoke.

My legs wrap around his waist as soon as he's on top of me. The heels of my feet against his ass and I'd love nothing more than to reach down and touch it, in fact, there isn't any part of him that I don't want to touch. His mouth crashes down on mine, his tongue sweeping in and I'm lost. That's all it takes from him, a kiss and I'm putty in his hands. I arch back when his finger enters me. His mouth still on mine, trailing his fingers along my body. His touch searing against my skin. It's too much, he's everywhere and yet, I don't want him to move. My body starts to grind against his finger and I feel his smile against my lips, thankfully he doesn't say anything.

My pleasure climbs and I'm grinding harder and harder against his hand. He tears his mouth away from me and I whimper, instantly missing the soul splitting kiss. "Give it to me, Kenna. Come for me." I shatter at his words, my breathing coming out in pants as I try and come down from the intense orgasm.

"I'm sorry, baby, but this is going to hurt," he murmurs. I should have prepared, but I was otherwise occupied. He slams his cock into me and pain tears me apart. I cry out and Dante stills inside of me. "I'm so fucking sorry." He holds me until I get accustomed to having him inside of me. I wiggle beneath him, testing to see if it still hurts. He lets out a sharp hiss. "Fuck, Kenna, I'm barely hanging on, don't do that again."

Instead of wiggling, I grind down against him, my pussy contracting around his thick cock. "Are you going to stay there all day?" I drawl, my legs tighten around his waist, "Or are you going to fuck me?"

"Christ," he growls but starts to move.

I've never known pleasure like it. Having Dante inside of me, filling me up, I feel something I never thought I'd feel. I feel like I'm home and that scares me. I push that thought out of my mind and focus on what's happening between us. "More… Harder," I beg, my fingers digging into his shoulders as I hold on.

"Makenna, I can't, I'm barely holding on…"

"Dante, do you think I give a shit if you lose control?" My fingernails dig into his shoulders as he thrusts into me harder than before. "God. Oh, please, Dante. I need more."

His mouth smashes against mine, and I know that he has finally released those reins he had. The kiss is hectic, hard, furious, and bruising. He continues thrusting into me and it's painful but the pleasure I'm feeling far outweighs the pain. I'm clawing at him as I try to reach that peak once again. It doesn't take long before that pleasure once again washes over me and I let go, screaming his name as my pussy spasms around his cock.

He thrusts, once. Twice. Three more times before he releases inside of me. "Fuck," he bites out, his breathing labored. He pulls out of me and lifts me into his arms. "Shower time."

"I can wash myself," I tell him although there's no heat in my words. "What the hell are you doing to me?" I ask once he sets me down on the counter in the bathroom.

He shakes his head. "Fuck, you're driving me crazy. You've gotten to me and I'm not sure I even want you there."

I laugh, at least I'm not the only one that's feeling this way. "You're stuck with me, so deal with it."

His eyes darken as his gaze sweeps across my naked body. "Oh, baby, you have no idea what you've gotten yourself into."

I smile, because I know exactly who Dante Bianchi is. The problem is, Dante has no clue as to who I am and that could be the biggest problem I've ever faced. "Shower time," I tell him as he turns it on.

"You're awake," I say as I walk into Alessio's room. I'm not sure where Romero is, I'd assume he'd have spent the evening in here with him. I've checked on Alessio every few hours and Romero wasn't in here any of those times.

He's frowning as he croaks, "I am. What the hell happened?"

I sigh as I walk over to him. "How much do you remember?" I lift up the blanket and check the bandage, there's no blood, which is fucking great, it means the stitches haven't busted.

His tongue darts out and he glances at me and then to the doorway, I know Dante's just walked in. "You got married, then all hell broke loose, I got shot…" His eyes move to my arm, "You got shot." I nod, he obviously knows what happened. "Then we came here and you were…" he glances down at my hand on his stomach, "and here I am."

I smile, "You passed out, either from the pain or the blood loss, I'm not sure which. You're fine, the bullet was taken out and it didn't hit anything major. You're all stitched up. The doc gave you antibiotics and a blood transfusion. You really shouldn't move for a couple of days and even then, it shouldn't be anything too strenuous."

A hand clamps on my waist, "What she means is, no fucking around. Once the doc has cleared you, then you can get back to work." Dante's voice is hard.

Alessio groans but nods. "Do you need anything? Angela's here, so if you're hungry, just let her know. For as long as we're here, she's going to be here." I turn, wanting to set some space between Dante and I. I know what's coming and I'm not ready for it.

"Thank you," he says and I nod.

I make my way toward my room and I smile when I see bags by the door. I arranged for Finn to get our things from the hotel and give them to Angela. At least this way, the men have some of their own things. I pick up the bag and walk into the bedroom, I instantly hear the door close behind me. Shit. Dante followed me.

"Okay, Makenna, I've had enough. It's time for us to talk."

I turn and face him, he's staring at me intently. He really does want me to bear all to him; unload all of my secrets. The problem with that is, it's giving him power. Power that I've never let anyone have before.

"Kenna, start talking."

"What do you want me to say?"

He takes a step closer to me. "I want to know exactly who I fucking married. I've done a lot of research on you and yet, staring at you now, I know that I don't have half the fucking info. So who the hell are you?"

I sigh, there's no way out of this. I open my mouth and decide to take a chance on a man that's made me feel things I shouldn't feel. If he betrays me, I'll kill him. I'm not the twelve year old girl who watched as her ma slit her throat, I'm stronger than that.

SEVEN

Dante

HER EYES close as I wrap my hand around her arm, careful not to hurt her. I'm still pissed she got shot yesterday, although, the way she's acting, it's like an everyday occurrence for her. She takes a deep breath and opens her eyes, they're void. Completely dead. I'm wondering what the fuck I've gotten myself into.

"I'm Makenna, that's the truth. I'm a Gallagher, albeit, a bit more than you were bargaining for. My da owns the Irish in New York, you already know that. But what you don't know is that he still answers to the Boss. Kind of like your da answering to the Capo dei Capi."

I get it, there's a Boss, over the Boss' it's the way it goes. It keeps the balance in the Mafia and also to try and keep the families at peace.

"Well my granda is the Boss, the real Boss. And he owns the Irish in America, all of them, along with Ireland, the UK, and Spain. My granda is the shit." She smiles and I can see the real love she has for him. "He's older than dirt but he's with the times. He makes decisions that he thinks work for the family. Some of those decisions have turned into secrets, and I'm privy to more than a few. Whereas, my da and brother's aren't."

I narrow my eyes, "Why would he tell you, but not your dad?" I have this sickening feeling that I've been played.

She shrugs and pulls out of my arms. "When I was twelve, I was hurt..."

I open my mouth to demand she tell me who the hell hurt her when she raises her hand quieting me down. I snap my jaw shut, grinding my teeth as I do so.

"I'll tell you that Dante, I will. But not today. You don't get all of my secrets today. I'll tell you most of them. But there are somethings I can't. Not yet. Not until..." She drifts off and I know that she meant she won't tell me until she knows if she'll be able to trust me or not.

"My throat got slit and Da lost his mind. He sent me away to live with Killian." She shakes her head with a smile. "Killian is gruff, he's not got kids and he doesn't have a wife, he lives for his cause and won't let anything get in the way."

"What cause is that?"

She frowns at me, there's a weird look in her eyes. "Dante, I thought you said you did your research?"

"I did," I say through gritted teeth. I don't think I've clenched my jaw as much as I have done in the past few minutes.

"Then you'd know that Killian is the leader of the American faction of the Real Irish Republican Army."

I blink, "Say what now?"

She bites her lip and my cock springs to life, "He's the leader of the Real IRA here in the US." She acts as though it's not a big deal.

"Your uncle is a fucking terrorist."

Her eyes flash with anger and annoyance. "Oh, listen here, you arsehole. He's not a terrorist. You don't see me classing you as one and you've probably killed as many people as he has. We don't get to judge people. We don't get to act superior to those that are in a similar line of work. We are all guilty of killing people."

"We?" I echo.

She nods. "Yes, we, Dante. Let me fucking finish the damn story," she snaps and I smirk, I definitely need her to get angry more often. The flash of those pretty green eyes, along with the way she purses her lips makes me hard. I wave my hand for her to continue. Heaven forbid I stop her.

"Thanks," she says sarcastically, rolling her eyes. "Da wanted me to be safe." She scoffs. "So he sent me away with Killian."

Christ, he sent her to live with that murdering asshole?

I don't know the man, I've heard the tales of what the IRA do and how they bomb innocent people and harm those that get in their way. Yes, the Mafia kills people, but we draw the line at innocent women and children.

"What Da didn't know was Killian thought it would be best to train me. So that's what he did. He taught me how to fight, how to shoot, and most of all, he taught me how to survive. To ensure that no one would ever be able to hurt me again."

Fuck, okay, maybe he's not a raging, murdering asshole.

"When he thought I was ready, he took me to Ireland where I spent most of my time with my granda. Did you know that I have another brother?" She laughs at my shocked expression. Fuck, how did we not know that she's got another sibling? "When Da was seventeen he met this woman, well, she was who he truly loved. She ended up getting pregnant and was sent away. Back in those days an unwed pregnant woman was a huge no-no. Granda wouldn't let Da marry her especially when Da was promised to Ma. So the woman had the baby and Da and Ma moved here and got on with their lives. Ma wouldn't let my brother, Denis, come stay with us. He was cut out of our lives and I don't think my other brothers know about him."

I reach up and push a stray strand of hair behind her ear, needing to touch her.

"So I spent the majority of my time with them. I'm a lot younger than Denis. He's got kids that are older than me and some that are younger. His wife is a bitch and I hate her, but I do love my nieces and nephews. So I stayed put. Granda had plans for Denis and I. We're his grandchildren, and with our family when you're in, you're in. So Denis runs Ireland, his son Danny runs the UK, and his other son Malcolm runs Spain."

"Your dad only runs New York. Who runs the rest?"

She looks at me and I know in that instant what her answer is. "I do..."

"Christ," I curse, what the fuck?

"Well, we do now." She drops that bomb with a little laugh.

"What?" I can't take my eyes off her, she's smiling, huge.

"Dante, I run the entire east coast other than New York. You are my husband, did you really think I'd not tell you who I really am and have you sit on the side lines? My men know that we're getting married and they also know that together we'll rule. Unless you have a problem with that?" There's a tone I don't miss, she's daring me to argue with her.

"You're fucking kidding, right?"

She sighs, "About what? Tell me what you think I'm joking about. Please, I really want to know."

"You think you can drop a bomb like that and everything is going to be okay?"

She moves so she's sitting on the bed. "Dante, grow the hell up and welcome to the twenty-first century. I am a woman, one that is more than capable of looking after herself, along with running the entire country if I wish. So you have a choice, be an arsehole, or be the Boss."

I curse her under my breath. I'm not fucking stupid. She'll fucking kill me, or I'll kill her. Damn, why the hell does the thought of her trying to kill me turn me on? Now I understand a hell of a lot more. Why she's been kept under wraps and it had nothing to do with her father. We're all her grandfather's puppets right now. He's the one that orchestrated this marriage, but what I need to know is why.

"Okay, so talk to me. What exactly do you do?"

She raises her brow, looking at me as though I'm a piece of shit and yeah, I probably am with the way I sarcastically asked her what she does.

"Do you mean how I own the drugs in the east? Or the fact that I have over sixty farms to grow that shit worldwide?"

I take my seat beside her on the bed, hoping she doesn't have a weapon on her. "Fuck, Kenna, this isn't how it's supposed to be."

She laughs, "Dante, do you honestly believe that if you had been given a docile woman you'd have been happy? Look at you, you're practically eye fucking me at every chance. Is it the fear of when I'm going to kill you that gets you off?"

I don't give into her bait, she's trying to get me off topic and that's not going to happen. "How many people have you killed?"

She shrugs, "More than I can count. I've been doing

this a long time. When you met me the first time, my granda had told me that when I returned to Ireland I'd be put to work. The first man I killed personally was for Kinsley, but I've ordered more than my fair share. Does this really bother you?"

It's my turn to laugh, "Not in the slightest. It's good to know that you can take care of yourself. But I hate that I was kept in the dark."

She nods, "That's good, I can work with that. If you did have a problem then it would get awkward. I've been through hell and back, Dante. Kidnapped, tortured, shot, you name it, it's happened. But I've survived and I'm not a weak woman that needs to be smothered. Try it and I'll smother you while you sleep. I can fight better than most men, because I need to show my men that I'm capable of the job. I can out shoot even the best snipers in the world and I can orchestrate a perfectly well thought out attack on someone in a matter of minutes. I've got men that are loyal to me. So much so that they work for me and haven't divulged my name. Anyone even tries and they'll die."

My respect for my wife has skyrocketed. "Okay, what do you want from me? You have a life, I don't understand why you needed me."

She rolls her eyes once again and I want to spank the shit out of her. "Dante, it's not about needing you. It's about bringing the Irish and Italian's together. It's about having someone who we can trust and be a part of our lives forever. Do I trust you? No, but I have to. So here it is. I've given you one of my biggest secrets, the one that you wanted to know and in doing so I'm showing you that I'm trusting you. Break my trust and I'll break your legs. Burn me and, Dante, I don't give a fuck who your family is. I'll slaughter the lot of you."

"Kenna, the moment I saw you in that fucking bar I

wanted to fuck you. Finding out that you were my fiancée made me go on a killing spree."

Her eyes widened, "It was you? You killed the Russians? I thought it was Ace."

"No, baby, that was me. He hurt you, so I ended him."

The smile she gives me now is softer than I've ever seen before. "Damn, Dante," she whispers as she wraps her arms around my neck.

"Fuck, baby, you don't do sweet do you?"

She shakes her head. "Nope, nobody's done anything like that for me."

"Get used to it. You're mine now, Kenna, and I'm not letting you go. That means, all of you is mine. All your secrets and all your dreams. Baby, I'm going to make sure you achieve whatever the hell it is you want."

"Fuck," she whispers, her voice raw and husky. "Dante, don't do this."

I slide my hand to her face, "Do what?" I ask, my mouth inches from hers.

I watch as she swallows hard, "Don't make me fall for you."

Fuck, having her love me isn't something I ever thought of, but I sure as fuck want it. "Tough," I say through a grin. "Things changed a hell of a lot tonight, Kenna, once I uncover all of your secrets, then I'll know that you've fallen for me."

I hear the sharp intake of breath all the way to my cock, "I don't know how to do this. I don't think I have the capability to love someone.

"Bullshit," I counter. "I know you do. You love Kinsley, you love your family."

"But they've been with me from the beginning." She makes it sound so simple.

"Doesn't mean you're not capable of it. I'm not asking you to love me, I'm just telling you to let me in."

She looks at me in wonder, "But, Dante, I have let you in."

I lean forward and kiss her. Her lips are plump and irresistible. "You have, to some degree. I'm not stupid, the things you've told me, you had to. We're married now, I was going to find out eventually."

She nods, "I don't think you're stupid. How about this? I'll tell you something that nobody on this earth knows?"

Like I'd turn that down? I don't know what it is about this woman but she makes me want to know everything about her. I want her more than I have anyone else and fuck if I know why her family have tried to protect her. She's sitting here, the sexiest woman I've ever had, probably the deadliest woman in the state, if not America. Yet as she looks at me, all I see is vulnerability. I know that if I tried to coddle her, as I would have done if she were different, she'd go for my balls. "Of course I want you to tell me."

"Kinsley is my best friend; she has been for as long as I can remember. We do everything together. She knows almost all of my secrets and I probably know roughly the same amount of hers. She told me that her grandfather was beating her and Ace. She was beaten to a pulp and I found her, she couldn't hide it, she was so bad. And honestly, I'm not sure if I hadn't found her would she have shared." I hide my smile when she crawls into my lap and rests her head against my shoulder, releasing a small yawn as she does. "Anyway, I had a plan in place. I'm in and out of the clubhouse just as much as Kinsley is. It's like a second home to me. Anyway, one night Ace came to see me, he said he needed my help."

I tense, wondering what the fuck he needed her help with.

"He wanted me to go to my da and ask him to take care of his grandfather for him. He told me to tell him, he'd owe him a marker. I said I'd ask and to leave it as that. His grandfather died the next day, his coke stash was shit."

"You asked your father?" I'm wondering where she's going with this.

She rests her hand against my chest, just as she did yesterday. "No, I didn't. I already had a plan, I poisoned his stash and waited. I couldn't let him hurt her anymore. To this day, Ace believes that my da was the one to kill his grandfather. Only you know that it was me."

Holy fuck. She killed the president of the Fury Vipers MC.

But he died years ago, meaning she got away with it.

Yet again, she surprises me, I thought she was done talking but I was wrong. "Sometimes, my heart races a little too fast. It's not that I'm scared or anything, it just races. I've never known how to make it stop until yesterday..." She confesses quietly. "I placed my hand right here..." She flexes her fingers on my chest, just over my heart and smiles. "I felt your heart beating and a calmness washed over me. It settled me."

I kiss her again, this time my hand gripping her thigh.

"Hurt me, Dante, and I mean it, I'll kill you."

I have no doubt in my mind that she would do it without losing an ounce of sleep.

"Same goes for you, baby."

She blinks, almost as if the mere thought of hurting me is incomprehensible.

I glide my hand up her thigh to her ass and squeeze, my other hand going to her hair and I pull her closer to my body. "I'm going to fuck you now. Then we're going to get food."

She smiles brightly. "I like your way of thinking." She nips my bottom lip. "Fuck me, Dante."

"My fucking pleasure," I tell her, slanting my mouth over hers and consuming her.

EIGHT

Makenna

MY STOMACH RUMBLES as I sit up. Dante's asleep on his front, his arm thrown over my stomach and his face turned into mine. I didn't intend to tell him about what I did to Kinsley's grandfather, nor did I plan on letting him know that he settles me. I don't trust Dante, I'm not sure if I'll ever be able to. But he's my husband and for some twisted reason, I feel safe around him.

I slide out of the bed trying not to wake him. God, the man is lethal, we spent our entire day in the bedroom and only came up for air when we needed food. Poor Angela has been waiting on all of us. Dante hasn't told me anything about his past and I shouldn't be surprised, but it's hurt me and I'm mad at myself for feeling this way. Alessio is still in bed; he's tried to move but I've warned him if he does, I'll shoot him again. He laughed and thought I was joking, until Dante told him I wasn't. He's assured me that he wouldn't try again, well at least until he's gathered more strength. Romero has been fixated on his laptop, I'm not sure what he's searching for but I'll have Dante find out for me.

"Sneaking out?" his amused voice calls out as I reach for my yoga pants. "Here I thought we'd gotten past this."

I roll my eyes, the man needs to relax. "This isn't a one-night stand, Dante, it's a marriage. I'm not sneaking out. I'm going to check on your brother and get some food. I'm starving. I also need to work today. My darling husband, fancy coming with?"

He chuckles, "Yeah, baby, why not."

I turn to face him, he's sitting up, the sheet around his waist showcasing his abs and muscles. "Don't sound so excited. Besides, today, I've got to meet up with Killian."

His face tightens and it pisses me off that he's made assumptions about my uncle without having ever met him. We don't get to criticize anyone, of all people, we don't have the right to judge. "Am I invited to that meeting?"

I should laugh at the pathetic attempt at acting as though he doesn't care, but I don't, I'm tired, annoyed, and hungry. "Sure." I pull on my tank top and move to the door.

A hand clamps around my waist, and spins me so that I'm facing him. "Want to let me know what's wrong?"

I sigh, "Why do you think anything's wrong?"

His eyes narrow at me, oh, looks like I'm pissing him off. "Your tone for starters. Fuck, Makenna, I'm not a damn mind reader, just tell me what the fuck is wrong."

I push him off me, "You are, arsehole. You expect me to tell you everything and yet, you haven't told me a damn thing about you. Now, I have to go and check on Alessio before he decides he's getting out of bed again. And while I'm doing that, maybe, you can check on Romero and see what he's looking for. Then I'm going to have some breakfast and go to Killian's, if you and your brothers want to come, you are more than welcome."

"Fuck!" he roars, but I ignore him and move down the

hall to check in on Alessio. I'm surprised to see Romero here.

"Morning," I say as I step into the room, their heads immediately come up and they both give me chin lifts. "How are you feeling today Alessio?"

He grunts and Romero laughs, "He's going stir crazy."

I nod as I walk over to the bed, checking on the bandage. "Do you want to try to shower?"

He looks relieved. "Hell fucking yes."

"Okay, but leave the door open and Romero will stay here in case you need help. Don't be stupid, if you feel your energy draining, call him. Otherwise you'll end up pulling your stitches out, which will mean being on bedrest for a while."

"Scouts honor." He grins and I laugh. I watch as he climbs out of the bed, I'm impressed with his speed, but he should be more careful.

"He's fine, Makenna," Romero says, not taking his eyes off the laptop screen.

I sigh, "Okay, well when you two are finished, we'll have breakfast and as long as Alessio hasn't busted his stitches open, you both can come with me and Dante today."

Romero raises his brow at me, probably wondering why I'm dishing out orders, but fuck him. It's my house and my life, I'll do whatever I want.

"I'll be in my office if you need me," I call out to them as I leave the room. The door to my bedroom is closed and I ignore the need to see him, I've given enough the past twenty-four hours. So much so, that I'm afraid of losing who I am.

Once I'm in my office, I make some phone calls, firstly, to Kins; I need to check to make sure she's okay.

"I'm good, Kenna, honestly. Ace got me out of there.

How are things going with you? Have you killed any of them yet?"

I laugh, "Not yet, although, the day has just begun."

"Are you okay?" Her voice is full of worry and I know that she's been stressing about it.

"I'm grand. I got nicked and it bled for a bit but it's fine. Dante was ever the gentleman last night."

I hear her name being called, "Shit, I've got to go. Call me later."

"Yeah, I need to get drunk."

She giggles, "Hell yes we do. Talk to you later, Kenna."

I hang up and listen, the shower's on which is a good sign. Hopefully Alessio is up for a day out, I need to get out of this house, I'm going stir crazy.

My cell rings and I glance down at the screen. Dad is calling.

"Hey, Da, everything okay?"

"That was my line," He grumbles. "We're all fine, we wanted to make sure that you were okay."

"I'm fine, Da, honest."

"Good, your uncle's here, and wants to talk to you." My da isn't much of a talker when others are around. Killian arrived late, he was supposed to be here a few days ago in time for the wedding, but he's only just arrived.

"Okay, I'll talk to you later, are we still on for Sunday?"

"Yes, and don't think you can come up with any bullshit excuses."

I smile, "I won't. Promise."

"Okay, Kenna, I'll talk to you later," he says and I wait until he passes the phone to Killian.

"Hey, kiddo, heard about yesterday."

I roll my eyes, he's the only one that calls me kiddo. "Yep, guess you were right."

He coughs, "I'm sorry, can you say that again?"

"No, fuck off, I'm not repeating myself. Your head is big enough as it is, I do not need to stroke your damn ego." I'm unable to keep the smile off of my face. That's one of the many things that I love about Killian, he knows how to cheer me up, even if it's by annoying the hell out of me.

"What was I right about?"

"That marrying the Italian would lead to a bloody wedding."

I hear a growl just as Killian laughs, glancing up I see Dante, Romero, and Alessio standing in the doorway looking at me.

"You never listen to me, Kenna."

I roll my eyes, "Hey, you're going on speaker." I wave them in, seeing as they're standing there and have no intentions of moving.

He grunts, "Is that Italian asshole there now?"

"Jesus Christ," I sigh, why does my family have to have so much hatred for the Italians?

"Makenna Gallagher, do not take the Lord's name in vain." Killain tries to sound stern but it doesn't work.

"God help me," I mutter. "Killian, no matter how hard you try, you and the Lord aren't ever going to be on good terms."

He scoffs, "You don't know that."

"When was the last time you went to confession?" His silence is enough of an answer for me. "Probably before I was born."

"Oh and tell me, wise one, when was the last time you confessed your sins?"

"Last week," I say with a smile.

"Fucking goody-two-shoes."

"Jealous much? Anyway, you wanted to talk to me?"

"Are you in a rush?" His voice is full of amusement, he's bored, and just wanting someone to annoy.

"Yes, I'm starving and I'm about to have breakfast. So what do you want?"

"Are you coming by later?"

I roll my eyes, what the hell? "Yes, I said I was, didn't I?"

"I was just checking, I wanted to make sure that Italian asshole hadn't tied you to the bed." I can hear the smile in his voice.

"He'd die if he tried. Now, is that all you wanted?"

"I'll set up the ring. Oh and Danny boy is here. He's eager to talk to you. I'll see you in a bit."

"Yeah, bye." I hang up and wonder why the hell Danny's in New York. Hell, why he's even in America at all.

"Who was that?" Alessio asks as I get to my feet.

"Her uncle." Dante answers for me and I raise an eyebrow, "I was listening to you."

I shrug, "We'll leave here soon enough. Are you okay to come?" I ask Alessio and he smirks, I'll take that as a yes.

"I was promised breakfast," Romero grumbles, obviously having had enough of the chatter.

"I was promised a husband, not his entire family, but hey, we all make sacrifices," I bitch back as I storm ahead and into the kitchen.

"Whoa, what the hell did you do to her?" Alessio questions and I'm not sure who he's talking to Dante or Romero. "Bro, she's going to kill you in your sleep," Alessio laughs.

"I know," Dante replies, making me smile, at least he knows.

"Good morning, Mrs Bianchi, I have eggs, bacon, sausage, and toast ready. Would you like a cup of coffee?"

I groan as I take a seat at the table. "Yes, please."

"Good morning, Mr Bianchi's. Can I get you coffee?" Angela asks with a smile as I send a text to Danny telling him to meet me at Killian's, and that I'll be there in an hour.

"That would be great, thanks, Angela," Dante replies and his brother's nod in agreement. "What time are we leaving?" he asks as he comes to sit beside me.

I resist the urge to kick him, but do glare at him. "Have other plans?"

He growls, running a hand through his hair. "Fucking hell," he mutters, then reaches for my chair and pulls me toward him. "I have six different ways to kill my father. Just waiting for the time to do so." He whispers in my ear. "I hate the man, Makenna, but seeing how he is around you, makes me want to slit his throat and be damned of the consequences."

We're not allowed to kill the Boss', if you're caught it means death. A long and painful death.

Angela brings us our coffees, and quickly follows it by putting plates in front of us. She quietly leaves the room, leaving us be.

"I want to rule, I want to be the Boss and, Makenna, before you, I'd have done so happily. Now, knowing what I know about you. It's going to be the two of us."

Now that is shocking. "Really?" I didn't think he had fully accepted that I am the Boss.

"Really, I also haven't told them who you are yet."

I smile, as I reach for my coffee. "Oh, today should be fun. Do they know who Killian is?"

He shakes his head. "Nope, but you can tell them when

we arrive." He reaches out and I shiver as his thumb lightly caresses my face. "I talked to Romero, he's been searching through the wedding footage to see if he can see anything."

I smile, that was on my to-do list this evening. "And?"

He shakes his head, "Nothing as of yet, but he feels as though there's something we're missing."

"Can I see the footage?" I ask turning my gaze to Romero who immediately gets to his feet and leaves the room. When he walks back in, he has his laptop tucked under his arm. He sets it down in front of me, taking the seat beside me. I press play, all of us watch as the scene unfolds, from me walking down the aisle, until Dante and I say I do and then all hell breaks loose. I rewind it again, and watch the man at the back, he hits the deck before Dante and I kiss. Well before the gunshot rings out.

I rewind it once again and press pause. I stare at the man, I haven't seen him before, I can name every one of the people that were there for me and me alone, but with my family and Dante's, our wedding was a huge event and there were a lot of people that attended that shouldn't have.

"Who's he?" I ask Dante, my finger pointing at the fucking arsehole.

"That's Kurt Holdsteader, he's a low level thug that works for the Famiglia. He actually cleans up a lot of mistakes that are made. He's been a part of our family for years. Hell, for as long as I can remember, Kurt has been a useful tool for us," Romero says with a smile. "He and Dad are friends."

"Yeah? Well look how fucking useful that bastard truly is." I hit play again and this time I know that everyone's eyes are on Kurt.

"Holy fuck. What the hell? He set it up?" Alessio growls.

"I'm going to kill him," Romero grunts in agreement.

"I'm going to enjoy making that asshole bleed." Alessio laughs and Dante shakes his head.

"Whoa, slow down there, chuckles," I tell him with a smile. "Why is it that men want to act first and think later?"

"Oh and tell me, genius, what is it that you suggest?" Romero glares at me.

It takes every ounce of strength not to reach for his throat, Dante's hand reaches for mine, holding on tightly. No doubt, he realizes just how close his brother is to losing his life.

"Well, obviously, Kurt didn't set it up himself. He's a low level thug. Which means someone set him up to do it, knowing that you'd find out and kill him, effectively ending the threat."

"Go on." Dante gives my hand a squeeze.

"So, what if we use Kurt? Find out who wants us dead and then take them out before they have a chance to take us out."

All of the men nod, "That's a good plan actually," Romero reluctantly admits.

"Who do you think would do this?" Alessio asks as everyone starts to eat their breakfast.

It's me that answers as I have no qualms in telling the truth. The Bianchi brothers have no idea who Dante married, but Dante trusts them and in turn I'll protect them. "I have a couple of ideas, but the ultimate question is, who's fucking brave enough to get into bed with the Bratva?"

"Fuck!" Dante slams his hand on the table, his jaw clenched, as pissed off vibes surround him.

Alessio and Romero start talking but Dante cuts through them.

"Eat, we'll figure this out. But now is the time to realize that you are alone. The only people you can trust are at this table and those alone can help us figure this shit out."

The silence hangs around the table, as we all contemplate the fact that we've at least two traitors in our midst.

NINE

Dante

I SEE the look in Makenna's eyes and realize that she's ready to kill someone. There's nothing I can do to calm her ass down. She was shot. Whoever orchestrated this shit, shot my fucking wife and almost killed my brother. Although, looking at Alessio you wouldn't know he was bleeding out yesterday.

"Ready?" I ask Kenna once we're all finished breakfast. She nods, and Romero gets up out of his chair. "Where are you going?"

He glances down at himself, he's wearing sweats and a t-shirt, something that we don't wear in public. "I need to get changed."

Makenna's shaking her head, "Nope, what you need to do is pack a change of clothes."

I smirk at the grimace that crosses Romero's face. He doesn't like taking orders at the best of times, and having Makenna do it is pissing him off but he does as she says and walks off, no doubt grumbling about her.

"What have you got planned?" I ask and realize that she's in a pair of yoga pants and an oversized sweater. She looks fucking sexy as hell, the pants showcase her phenomenal ass.

She shrugs and smiles, "I'm not sure what you mean." She leans forward and kisses my lips. It's quick and brief but fuck if it doesn't mean something. "Alessio, are you sure you're okay to come?"

She seems to have a soft spot for him, where she rides Romero, she babies Alessio.

He rolls his eyes, "Yes, fuck, I'm not an invalid."

Her eyes narrow at his tone, "I never said you were, I asked a question." She sighs heavily before turning back to me, "Oh and Sunday, we're having dinner with my family."

I blink, "Why the fuck are we having dinner with them?"

"Because…" she says slowly. "They're my family and every Sunday we have dinner together. It's the only day that we ever spend together. I've missed a lot. So, you're coming, and you'll be the buffer."

I raise my brow, "Buffer between who?"

She grins and it's fucking sexy yet satanic. "Between me and my mother." She rubs her scar on her throat and it's in that moment that it hits me. She's never told anyone about what happened to her that night. But she hates her mom, more than I think she hates anyone. But she loves the rest of her family, all of them.

"Alessio," I growl. "Go and see if Romero needs anything." I dismiss him and without question he gets to his feet and leaves the room. As soon as we're alone. "She did this to you." It's not a question.

"Leave it, Dante, please?"

I swallow hard, my head pounding as blood rushes from it. Fire fills my gut and all I see is red. I've never been so fucking angry before. "Kenna…" My voice is hoarse and tight. "I'm asking you to please, tell me what happened."

She scowls at me. "Fuck you, Dante." She whispers, "Why are you doing this to me? Hmm, do you get a fucking kick at trying to rip away at my walls?"

"Those walls you've built are fucking so high no-one can get in. I'm going to break them down one by one and, Makenna, when they're down, you're going to be mine. Now, tell me what happened."

She growls and turns away from me, "I heard a noise and went to investigate. I was used to one of my brother's coming home hammered and stumbling all over the place. I used to help them to their rooms and make sure they were okay before going back to my room."

Anger flares in my veins. She's been taking care of everyone and yet no-one takes care of her. That shit's about to change.

"But it wasn't one of my brother's. The sound was coming from my parents' room." She shakes her head, "I ignored it and went downstairs to get a drink, disregarding it as my parents having sex." She scrunches up her face in disgust and I bite back my smile. "But when I went back upstairs I realized it wasn't my da that was with her."

Fuck, her mom was having an affair? Her dad mustn't know otherwise he'd have gone mental. Women are meant to be faithful. In our world it's a death sentence to cheat on your husband. When Makenna turns back to face me, the look she has on her face makes me brace. Whatever she's going to say, I'm not going to like.

"I saw the man, he saw me and he fucking hated that I'd seen them together. I heard what he said to her. He told her that she had to get rid of me, that if my father found out it would mean a war between the families. Mom pleaded with him and that's when he came into the hall."

She balls her hands up into fists and I watch as the anger flashes through her eyes. "He punched me, told me that I should have been a good girl and stayed in my room."

I'm going to fucking kill him, I don't care who it is, he's going to die.

"He kept hitting me until mom cried out and told him to leave before my da got home. I was lying on the floor and all I kept thinking was he's going to kill me. But what shocked me the most was that he didn't. Instead he told mom that she had a choice, she could get rid of me or he'd tell Da what happened." She shrugs, "Mom made her choice, she wanted to protect herself, her marriage, so she told him she'd get rid of me. She'd never hurt someone before, it was new for her. So she messed up when she slit my throat, she didn't do it properly."

I stare at her in wonder, how is she so fucking blasé about this? Her mom tried to kill her because the cunt was having an affair and rather than protect her child, she took the coward's way out and tried to kill her own daughter.

"I started to choke, she cut my throat too low, so the wound bled a lot. Thankfully Finn came home and mom hid in her room, pretending to be fast asleep. He got to me in time and I was okay."

I slam my hand against the table and she gets to her feet. "You're not okay!" I yell, fucking pissed that she's acting as though this is normal. "Who? Who was your mom fucking that made her try and kill her own daughter?"

She shakes her head, her arms crossed over her chest. "You've heard enough, Dante. Leave it be now."

I move, stalking across the room until we're face to face. My chest heaving as I try and tamper down my anger.

"Kenna, I'm fucking asking as your husband, who gave your mom the order?"

She licks her lips and turns her head away from me, I grip her chin with my hand and pull it so that she's facing me. "Makenna, I'm not going to ask again. Who?"

"Your father," she whispers and my entire body freezes. What the fuck? "Dante, you're father wanted this wedding to fuck with me. He thinks I'm a beaten down girl that he can fuck with, but I'm not."

I can't fucking believe this shit. My anger is bubbling to the surface. I move back a step, releasing her and ramming my fist into the wall above her head. She doesn't flinch, she stands there watching me. There's no fear, there's nothing.

"Kenna, I'm not going to hurt you," I tell her softly and she blinks.

"I know, I'd kill you if you even tried." Her voice is even, she's not moved an inch and I fucking hate that she's this cold. I frame her face with my hands, she blinks at me, a furrow between her brows. "What are you doing?" she asks, confused.

"You're my wife, Makenna, I'm not going to hurt you and I'm not going to let anyone fuck with you. I told you about my plans for my father and knowing he's done this to you, I'm not waiting any longer."

She places her hand on my chest, right above my heart. Her touch is gentle and I remember back to our conversation last night where she confessed that it settles her. I kiss her lips softly and she opens her mouth for me. I sweep my tongue into her mouth and love that it sets her off, her hand on my chest flexes and she brings the other to my hair and tugs.

"Dante, as much as I'd love to have you fuck me here against the wall, your brothers are probably outside the door waiting for us and I'm not going to fuck you where they can walk in and see."

Talking about my brothers is like having an ice cold bucket of water thrown over me. I release her and take a step backward, needing to put a bit of distance between us before I do fuck her.

"I don't know what it is about you, Dante, but keep going and you may just get your wish." She murmurs as she walks past me, snatching up her cell phone off of the kitchen table as she does.

"Arseholes," she grumbles as she walks out the door. I smile when I realize she was right, Romero and Alessio are standing outside the door as soon as she's out of the kitchen they enter.

"How much did you hear?"

Romero's eyes are dark and filled with anger. "All of it. Fucking bastard," he grunts. "I never took him as a coward, if he wanted her dead, he should have fucking done it himself. Now? He's trying to torture her."

Alessio grins, "So, you get off on her threatening you?"

"Fuck off," I tell him as I move toward the door.

"Want to tell us what the hell is up with that woman? I mean, she's unlike any other woman I've ever known. She's strong, she's got some guts bossing me around. If she weren't your wife I'd have finished the job her mom couldn't."

I hear her laughter, feminine and husky. "Oh, Romero, you wish you could." She's standing in the doorway with her arms crossed over her chest, glaring at him.

His eyes flash and I decide it's time to step in. These two are going to kill each other eventually. "It's time to go." I reach for her and pull her into my body. She tries to push me away but I hold on tight and she sighs, twisting around so that she's facing forward.

"Where are we going?" Alessio asks as we move toward the elevator.

"We're going to see my uncle," Kenna tells him. "It's been a while since I've seen him."

Once we're in the elevator, she presses her hand against the panel, which begins our descent to the garage. She walks to the driver side and climbs in. Alessio and Romero climb into the back, all the while Romero glaring at the back of her head. I sigh, it's like having fucking children with these two. Once I'm inside the car, Makenna drives out of the garage, the sunlight beaming through the window making her hair shine. I put my seatbelt on because Kenna's a fucking menace behind the wheel. I'm not sure if she understands the concept of speed limits.

Ten minutes into the car ride her phone rings, the sound blaring through the speakers, she must have it hooked up through Bluetooth. "Hey, Kenna." Kinsley's voice says through the speakers. "Are you busy?"

I watch as Makenna frowns, "I'm driving, I'm going to Killian's and you're on speaker."

"Who's with you?"

Her frown deepens, "Dante and his brothers. What's going on?"

There's silence. "Okay, so last night, shit hit the fan," Kinsley tells her and I see Makenna sit up straighter. "Ace, Stag, and Benny went crazy, they found out what dad was doing."

"About fucking time. Please, tell me that arsehole is dead?" Makenna responds as her body begins to relax.

"Yep, and get this. Dad? He wasn't our actual dad. When mom was pregnant with me, our dad died and she and Jaws got together. Plus as vice president, Jaws became president and nobody said anything. Until last night."

Holy fuck, I guess it's been a fucking twenty-four hours

for revelations. How the hell did none of my research uncover the fact that Julian 'Jaws' Montry wasn't Kinsley's dad? Hell, none of my research was any way useful and now that I know about what happened to Makenna I understand why. My father. He's going to die a slow and painful death.

"So the asshole is dead?" Makenna says looking in the rear-view mirror.

"They both are. Ace went ape shit. I'm telling you, Makenna, I've never seen anything like it. It was a massacre."

Makenna pouts, "He couldn't wait?"

Kinsley groans, "Makenna Bianchi, are you pouting?" Her question is met by silence as Makenna glances at me. "You're pouting because you didn't get to join in?"

The smirk on Makenna's face tells me that's exactly why she was pouting. "Fine, I wanted to kill that bastard. So, Stag, huh?"

"Yeah, he claimed me last night," Kinsley says and Makenna smiles. "Anyway, I wanted to let you know what happened last night, I'm good Kenna, honest."

I watch as Makenna bites her lip, a barrage of emotions etched on her face. "Yeah?" Her voice is soft.

I glance back at my brothers. They both have worried expressions on their faces as they look at Makenna, neither of them can see her face, but they're obviously worried.

"Yeah, no more having to save me. You were right. When it started to happen I should have told Ace. If I had, it wouldn't have gone on for as long as it has," Kinsley replies and it's even more secrets that I need to uncover. "Maybe you should tell your dad about what happened."

Makenna laughs, "Yeah, that's not going to happen. Could you imagine how Da will react when he finds out that not only is his wife a whore but she also tried to kill his only daughter?"

So Kinsley knew what happened and she kept that a secret? What the fuck? Who does that shit?

Kinsley gasps, "Kenna, babe, you're not alone."

Kenna sighs, "Yeah, I told Dante this morning and his brothers overheard. Nosey bastards."

Kinsley laughs, "I'm surprised that Dante let you up for air. He looked like he wanted to eat you alive yesterday."

Romero chuckles and Makenna grins. "There's always later." She winks at me, "I've got to go, I'm almost at Killian's. You coming?"

Kinsley groans, "No, Stag doesn't want me to leave the clubhouse, he's worried that killing that asshole could start a fucking war. So far though, the other brothers are on board. It's the other chapters they've got to convince."

Makenna shakes her head. "Fuckers. Let me know if you need any help."

"Yeah, I said it to Ace last night. He wanted to kill you." She laughs, "I told him he could try but he does want to talk to you. Oh by the way, he knows about you."

Makenna frowns, "Knows what about me?" Because there's so many fucking secrets.

"He knows what you are. Kenna, I didn't tell him. I swear, he figured it out last night while we were talking."

"Kins, I have no idea what you're talking about. He knows what?"

"About your job." Kinsley tells her, "Shit, I've got to go."

Fuck, just how many people know that she's the Boss? And how the hell did we not?

Kenna giggles, "Tell Stag I said hello."

I can hear the hushed voices, "Tell me yourself when

you get your ass to the club. Just 'cause you're married don't mean we don't miss you," the deep baritone voice says. This must be Stag.

Makenna's laugh is louder, "Okay, I'll swing by tomorrow. Oh and Stag, hurt her and I'll kill you."

He doesn't laugh like I assumed he would. "Not gonna happen, Kenna. I know what you've done for her and I'm grateful. I owe you, girl, more than I'll ever be able to repay. You need me, I'm there. But you don't have to worry about Kins, I've got her now."

The softness in Makenna's eyes tells me that she believes him. "Okay, Stag, I'll see you tomorrow."

"Alright, girl. See you then."

The call ends and Makenna grins. "You ready for this?" she asks me. I nod in response. Her uncle is a fucking terrorist but what the fuck? I married the head of the Irish Mafia.

She turns into what can only be described as a fucking castle. It spans the entire width of land that it sits on. At least a hundred windows face us as she drives up the long drive toward it. The Irish flag displayed proudly on the rooftop blowing in the wind. Makenna parks the car and slides out, a fucking beautiful smile on her face as she turns to face us.

"Gentleman, welcome to the New York headquarters of the RA." Her Irish accent is thick as she pronounces the word RA, which I know some Irish use as short for the IRA.

"The what?" Romero asks and Makenna laughs as he walks up the steps.

"Well if it isn't my favourite bloodthirsty niece." A man who looks identical albeit slightly younger than Seamus grins and pulls her into his arms.

She glares at him. "Don't let Jade hear you say that."

He just grins at me, "you tells us all we're your favourite, don't you?"

He just laughs, but it answers her question. He does. "Come on in, everyone's waiting to see the Italian."

"Killian, don't piss me off," she tells him, her voice stern as she continues to glare at him.

"Fine," he grunts as though he's been reprimanded. "Come in." He invites us and walks away.

"Someone want to tell us where the hell we are and who that asshole was?" Romero asks his hand twitching for his gun.

"That arsehole is my uncle. Killian Gallagher. He's also the head of the IRA, here in New York." She drops that bomb with a smile. "Welcome gentleman."

"Son of a bitch," Romero growls.

"She really is going to kill you, isn't she?" Alessio says with a grin. "She's connected, fucking hell that woman probably has more contacts that we do."

I sigh, scrubbing a hand down my face. "You have no fucking idea." I take the steps two at a time as I get ready to enter the lion's den.

TEN

Dante
___

AS I ENTER THE HOUSE, I see Kenna waiting for me. My brothers walk in behind me. "Ready?" she asks and I can feel the excitement bouncing off of her.

"Yep, the sooner we get this shit over with the better."

"Yeah, just what we need, to be in bed with terrorists," Romero growls.

Makenna spins on her heel and pierces him with a vicious glare. "Listen to me, arsehole, because I'm only going to say this once." Her voice is low as she takes a step closer to him. "You do not get to judge people on what they do, how many men have you killed?" When Romero doesn't answer she advances on him again. "How many women and children have you murdered?"

"It's not the same," he tells her through gritted teeth.

"Oh and why not? Because you think you're a fucking god? The IRA have a cause, one that they believe in and will do anything for. Just as you do with the Famiglia. Just as I do for the Clann. It's the way it goes. Next time you disrespect my family, I'll end you. Dante won't be able to stop me, do I make myself clear?" The huskiness of

Makenna's voice mixed with the anger she has makes my cock stir. Why is it that she fucking affects me like no other?

He glares at her and I'm shocked as shit that he just nods, "Yes, Boss."

What the fuck? How the hell did he know that shit?

"Kenna, Danny boy wants to talk to you," her uncle shouts from further in the house. Makenna sighs and walks toward the sound of Killian's voice.

When I turn to follow it's then that I realize there's at least a dozen men here. All of them stand a little taller as Makenna walks past them.

"Bro, what the fuck? You called her *Boss*," Alessio hisses. "Are you fucking crazy?"

Romero huffs, "No, but I think Dante might be." He turns to me, "When were you going to tell us? Hmm, that you married the head of the fucking Irish Mafia?" He's a smart fucker. Always has been.

"I only found out last night myself. Her father and brothers don't know. When she was sent away, she was made into a fucking killer."

Alessio scoffs, "How bad can one woman be?"

Romero shakes his head. "You've no fucking idea. You don't understand what it means to have Makenna as the Boss, do you?"

"Makenna is the head of the Irish Mafia on the east coast, all of it, except for New York," I explain to them both, still fucking coming to terms with it myself. I need to see what she can do, if she's not able to protect herself then I'm going to have to train her.

We manage to catch up to them, I step in line beside Makenna with my brother's walking beside me. Killian a few steps ahead of us. "Where is he?" Kenna asks as we walk toward the room at the back of the house.

"He's on the phone," Killian says. These fucking Irish

are hard to understand when they get together; Makenna's accent gets thicker.

"Why is he here?"

Killain shrugs, "I've no idea, I asked the boy that myself. Do you know what the little shit said to me?"

Makenna rolls her eyes, "No, but I'm sure you're going to enlighten us."

Killian shakes his head, a smile playing on his lips. "You always were a little shit. He told me that I wasn't in the know and to mind my own business. No fucking respect," he says with a shake of his head. There's no heat in his words, "How bad is your arm?"

Makenna waves him off, "It's fine, just a graze, didn't need stitches."

His gaze moves from Makenna to Alessio, "And you?"

"Fine," Alessio replies with a grunt and Makenna pins him with a glare. "I'm alive, thanks to Makenna."

Killian nods, "She's good. But we're going to see how good you Bianchi's really are." His eyes sweep through the three of us. "I take it you're the lucky one that she chose for this," he says to Romero with a grin.

Romero glances at Makenna with a glare and her response? To smile sweetly at him. "And what exactly did she choose me for?"

Killian grins and opens the door in front of us, "You're about to see."

When the door is open fully, I see a boxing ring in the middle of the room. There's at least thirty men here, all of whom turn to face us when we enter.

"Follow me and for the love of God, do not look down. Keep your head held high," she says, her gaze on Alessio. She strolls into the room and I keep in step beside her. Her stride is full of purpose; she's working the room like she owns it. Every man in this room has respect for her.

"Boss?" I hear a man call out.

Makenna's steps don't falter. "Talk to me after Michael, make sure your son is in attendance," she tells the man, not even looking at him.

My gaze lands on the man and I see the smile on his lips, what she said is what he wanted to hear. "Yes, Boss, and congratulations on your nuptials."

That gets a smile from her. "Appreciated," she murmurs as she reaches for my hand and we stand in front of the boxing ring. "For those that don't know, I got married yesterday." There are some nods, a few murmurs, but mostly keen gazes. "I'd like for you to meet my husband Dante Bianchi."

I give them a nod, not saying anything, this is her show… For now.

"If you have a problem, you come to one of us. He and I are as one. Now, do you have any questions?"

"Yeah, Boss, I do." A man steps forward, he must be in his late thirties, early forties. He's got jet black hair and is wearing a suit, one of the very few here to be in one. Makenna motions for him to carry on. "You're marriage to the Bianchi, does that mean that the Italian's and the Irish will be joining forces?"

Makenna glances at me and smiles, "Want to take this one, love?"

I roll my eyes at the endearment, it doesn't suit her. "Sure, baby," I murmur and her lips twitch. "As soon as my father is no longer Capo, I will be and in turn, Makenna will be. That means that my men and Makenna's men will be our men. Anyone who has a problem with that let us know now."

Makenna's smile widens, "Exactly what my husband said. We are building something here, gentleman, and it's something that we've worked hard for. We've known for five years that this day would come and we knew what it would mean."

The men nod again. "Boss, what about your father?" the same man says and the glances of the other men get nervous.

"That's a conversation between us, but he'll be brought up to speed with what's happening."

"He'll also have to be informed that from now on he answers to you." I turn my attention from the crowd to the voice and see the newcomer standing in the doorway, his arms crossed over his chest and smiling as he looks at Makenna. The fucker's tall, over six-feet. Tattoos cover his arms, as well as one on his neck.

"Fucking hell, Danny boy, I told you to tell her that shit in private." Killian groans and climbs into the ring.

"Any more questions?" Makenna says ignoring the man. "That doesn't involve my father?"

"What about the other men?"

Makenna nods, "Next week we'll hold a meeting. Every *made man* is to be in attendance. If they're not, there will be hell to pay. Do I make myself clear?"

A chorus of 'Yes, Boss' goes around the room.

"Good, now those who are staying for the show, do. Those that aren't, leave," she instructs and a dozen or so men leave, bidding her a farewell and giving me a chin lift in respect. This went a hell of a lot better than I had expected.

She glares at me. "This may have seemed easy, Dante, but it won't be. Those were my Underbosses and they aren't disrespectful. Well not in front of you. If they have concerns I'm going to hear about it. The *made men* are a different problem altogether. Some of them resent the fact that I'm a woman, others because I'm a hell of a lot younger than them, and some are a mixture of the two. It doesn't matter how many times I prove myself, they're not going to like it and now having an Italian husband is going to add more fuel to the fire."

I pull her into my arms and her glare turns feral. "Fuck, Kenna, don't look at me like that, you make me want to fuck you against the nearest wall." Her eyes dilate at my words, "Now, what are you going to do if someone disrespects you?"

"I'll kill them. Just as you would." There's absolutely no hesitation in her words. It's great that she has the talk, but can she actually go ahead with it?

She pulls out of my arms and smiles, "Now, if you don't mind, I have shit to do."

She turns back to her men and smiles. "Who's up first?"

A man steps forward, he's about Alessio's age, he pulls his top off and climbs into the ring.

"Romero, you're up," she tells him and I watch as Romero gives her his shark's grin. "Romero, these men are looking to tear you apart. You are a Bianchi, but you are also my brother in law. Do not fucking let me down."

His grin gets bigger. "Don't worry, *sis*. I've got this." She raises her brow at him. "Trust me."

"I do, that's why I chose you."

He pulls off his top and he too climbs into the ring. Killian wraps Romero's hands as Danny wraps up the Irish man's.

"Good luck, Bianchi." The man spits at Romero and Makenna's eyes narrow. "Sorry, Boss, I forgot you were one now."

"Jared," she warns and he nods.

Killian rings the bell and the two circle one another. Jared throws the first jab, one that Romero easily dodges. It's quickly followed by a combination shot. Again Romero dodges them, and finally throws his own, catching Jared on the jaw as he does. Jared stumbles and Romero ever the hunter, pounces, throwing more jabs. It doesn't take long for Jared to crumble to the floor.

"Jared, out, Harrison, you're in," Makenna calls, not once taking her eyes off the ring. Jared gets to his feet and climbs out of the ring looking pissed.

Romero makes light work of the next three guys, with each new contender his ego grows as does his grin. When he sends the guy he's boxing to the canvas, Makenna takes off her sweater and reveals that she's only in a fucking sports bra. She discards her sweater on the floor.

"What the fuck?" I growl as she climbs into the ring and Danny starts to tape her hands up.

Romero's gaze comes to me, the confusion clear on his face. He knows if he touches her I'll kill him.

Makenna throws the first jab and it clips Romero's jaw, he didn't block fast enough. She doesn't relent, she moves forward, jabbing him twice in the stomach before dancing away out of his reach. The room is silent, as we wait to see what's going to happen. Will he fight back or is he going to keep letting her hit him?

Makenna keeps going for him, the sound of her fists against his skin is unrelenting. Jab after jab, she doesn't stop. When she catches Romero's jaw again, I know that he's had enough. He punches back and she dances away from his fist, laughing as she does. Each time she hits him, she moves quickly away from him. She's fucking fast, he's unable to get her and it's something I never thought I'd see. Romero is one the best fighters I've seen. Until now.

I'm not sure how long it goes on for, Makenna's jabs come hard and fast. She doesn't even look out of breath, not even a sheen of sweat on her face. Not for the first time I wonder who the fuck I married. She fights better than any man I know, she can shoot straight, she drives like she's been stealing cars since she was a child. Every time I think I'm starting to get to know her, she shocks the shit out of me with something else.

"Enough," Killian says coming into the ring and stopping the fight. "Romero, you put up a good fight." He laughs. "Get out of the ring," he instructs. "Danny boy, you're up next."

Romero climbs out of the ring and walks over to Alessio and I, he pulls his shirt on. "Fucking hell, you could have warned me," he grunts and I can tell he's in pain.

"Tell you what, exactly?"

"That your wife is a fucking bitch. Christ, I think she hit my kidney. I'm going to be pissing blood."

I bite back my smile as I watch Killian tape Danny's hands. Makenna reaches for a gum shield. I'm going to fucking spank her ass. She didn't wear one while in the ring with Romero. One punch and he could have shattered her jaw.

The fight between them begins and it doesn't take me long to realize that my wife was going easy against Romero. The punches she's throwing now are hard and the sound against Danny's skin is monstrous. She's a fucking animal in there. Danny's giving it as good as he's getting; he's returning it hard. She manages to out dodge most of them, a few slamming into her midsection. She doesn't even flinch, instead, she powers through and slams into his nose. The sound of bone crunching makes me smile.

"Stop fucking playing around and end it," Killian yells over the grunts.

Makenna pouts but nods and her punches become ferocious. Her combinations are on point, one into the jaw, the next into his stomach, followed by one to the temple.

Danny's ass hits the canvas and the cheers go up around the room. Killian hops into the ring, his grin wide as he looks at Makenna with pride. He trained her, and he obviously did a fucking good job.

The room clears instantly; the men have seen what the Boss can do and now it's time to get their asses back to work.

"Christ," Danny groans as he gets to his feet. "Who the hell have you been training with?"

Makenna laughs and helps him to his feet. "Hayden."

Danny's eyes narrow, "That prick?"

Makenna's laugh rings out through the room. "Yes, he's your cousin. Isn't it time to get over it?"

"No. It's not. He fucked me over."

Makenna climbs out of the ring once she's got the tape off her hands, "You were both fifteen. Get the hell over it. Stupid idiots, trying to fight over the same damn woman. I don't understand why you're so pissed. Hayden ended up catching the clap."

Danny laughs, "Shit, I forgot about that. You're right. I should forgive him. Especially if he's training you. I thought he was in Chicago?"

Makenna walks over to me, a bright smile on her face. I can't help but be fucking proud. "He is in Chicago."

He narrows his eyes, "When the hell were you in Chicago?"

I watch as she counts to three, her eyes narrowed into slits. "Danny—" Her voice is dangerously low and I see him take a step backward. "You are not my father, nor are you my husband. I am old enough to make my own decisions and I can go where I damn well please."

"Auntie Kenna," he says softly as he moves toward her.

She spins and pins him with a glare, "Don't try and flatter me."

He grins, "You're my favourite auntie."

She sighs, "You and Killian are the fucking same. I am your only auntie. You cannot sweet talk me." She turns to face me. "I'm going to have a shower before I kill my nephew. Please, while I'm gone, resist doing it for me."

I chuckle, "I'll try, no promises though." She raises up to her tip-toes to kiss me. Her tits press against my body and my cock stirs.

"Down boy," she whispers as she walks away from me, her body swaying as she does.

"Fucking hell, how many secrets does she have?" Alessio asks once we're alone.

"Um, want to explain how she has a nephew that's older than her? None of her brothers have had kids?" Romero asks and winces. "Fuck, she can really land a punch."

I bite back a laugh, "If you want, I'm sure she can train you."

Alessio throws his head back and laughs.

"So, what are we going to do about dad?" Romero questions quietly.

Now that's a good question. Right now I have no idea. It needs to be executed perfectly. The last thing I need is for anyone to find out I killed him. I have so many different ways of killing him, all of them wouldn't lead back to me.

I'll talk it over with Makenna, that woman has a fucking terrifying mind and no doubt will have the perfect way to kill the bastard. His time is coming and when it does, I am going to be the one to end his life.

ELEVEN

Makenna

I WALK DOWNSTAIRS after getting washed and dressed. Killian still kept some of my clothes here, which I'm not surprised. As much as he likes to act like he doesn't care, he really does. He always makes an effort to check in every so often. I'm the closest thing he has to a child and I love him just as I love my da.

"Kenna?" Danny calls as I hit the bottom step. I turn at the sound of his voice. He's got tape over his bloody nose, bruising is already starting to form underneath his eyes, and he's gingerly standing by the door, favoring his left side. The blow to his abdomen must have hurt him.

"Yeah, Dan, what's wrong?" When I first found out about Denis, I thought it was weird that he had children that were older than me. Danny is the oldest, he's a few years older than me but still has the mischievous look to him. He runs the UK while Denis runs Ireland, the two of them have an iron fist with how they rule and nobody messes with them.

"I fucked up Kenna," he says softly as I walk over to him. "Da's going to fucking kill me when he finds out."

Pinching the bridge of my nose, I grimace, just knowing this isn't going to be good. "What the hell did you do?" The relationship that Denis has with his kids is strong, he'd do anything for them.

He sighs, raking his hand through his hair. "I fucked Melissa Harding." Melissa is the illegitimate daughter of Graham Harding, the head of the Harding Gang in London. She's off-limits, as is their entire family. Him sleeping with her is going to start a war.

My eyes widen. "What the fuck?" I screech, my fingers itching to reach out and snap his neck. I take a step away from him, killing my nephew isn't going to go down well. "Please, tell me that you are joking?"

Dante, Romero, Alessio, and Killian all step into the hall, their eyes glancing from me to Danny.

"Kenna, I fucked up, what do you want me to say?" He's pissed now, he stands back against the wall and crosses his arms over his chest. He's trying to look intimidating. Not happening.

"You fucked up? Danny, you didn't forget to pick up the dry cleaning. You didn't crash the car. You fucked Melissa Harding. You fucking moron."

"It was an accident," he lamely replies.

I scoff, "Oh, let me guess, she tripped and her vagina just happened to land on top of your dick? You being the upstanding gentleman that you are, moved to help her, only to thrust into her?"

Killian throws his head back and laughs, I turn my glare onto him. What the hell is wrong with Danny?

"Did you know about this?" I ask Killian.

His laughter dies instantly. "Fuck no. If I did, I wouldn't have told him to come here. I'd have told him to go to Australia." *Of course he would.*

"Makenna," Danny says softly and I turn my attention back to him. "That's not even the worst part of it."

I sigh as I close my eyes. "She's pregnant." It's a statement, but he nods anyway. "Are you sure it's yours?" Again he nods, "Then you're going to have to marry her."

"Not fucking happening," he says through clenched teeth. "We're in the fucking twenty-first century, Makenna. I'm not marrying that psycho bitch."

I take a step forward and he stands his ground. "You should have thought about that before you let your fucking dick call the shots. What the hell were you thinking?"

"He wasn't, that's the problem," Killian inputs and Danny glares at him.

"Danny, does Zack know yet?" I ask, wondering how much time we have before shit hits the fan. Zack is a fucking psychopath, he's going to go postal when he finds out what's happened.

I hear the sharp intake of breath and turn to Romero, "Dude, you fucked *and* impregnated Zack Harding's sister?" He lets out a low whistle. "Damn, he's going to kill you."

"Why haven't you told your da yet? Does Granda know?" I ask, ignoring Romero's commentary.

"No, as soon as I found out I came here. Well I was already coming here…"

"You mean you legged it. Fucking hell," I mutter. He's up shit creek without a paddle right now. "You're going to have to marry her. It's the only way you're going to stay alive."

"Well, I was hoping that you'd…"

I cut him off with a shake of my head. "Oh no, you messed up, Danny boy, I am not going to war over your dick!"

"Shit," he curses as he runs his hands through his hair

again. "What do I do?"

"Stupid and deaf," I comment, causing him to narrow his eyes at me. "Don't look at me like I'm the bad guy, I'm not. I'd do anything for you, you know that. But I can't do this. You could have had any other woman, why her?"

I see the spark in his eyes and I shake my head. "Don't, I don't want to hear you say it was for the challenge."

"Makenna's right, not only that, she's actually being smart. She's giving you the chance to go home and put that shit into motion before your da or granda finds out. It'll show them that while you fucked up, you also have your head on right to rectify those mistakes."

"Fuck!" Danny roars, "I can't do it, Makenna, she's a fucking psycho, I hate that bitch."

I shrug, "If you hate her you shouldn't have stuck your dick in her. Sorry, but there's no other choice. You either do it of your own free will or, Granda and Denis will get involved and, Danny, they'll not be so nice about it."

Romero chuckles, "Nice? This is what you call nice?"

I glare at him, "I didn't strangle him, did I?"

Now Danny chuckles, "Oh but you wanted to. Don't think I didn't notice your fingers itching to get a hold of me."

"Your fingers twitched this morning too," Dante says with a smile. While *I* start repeating *do not kill anyone* over and over in my head. "You wanted to kill Romero."

"We're Irish, we have a short fuse and an impossible temper," Killian explains.

"Look, Danny, you've got to make a choice. I can't make it for you."

"Although you'd like to."

"You're older than me, you should have known what was going to happen when you fucked her. This is your mess, sorry, but you're the only one that can fix it."

He groans, "A bullet in her head would be too much?"

I smirk, "A little overkill, don't you think? Look, see it this way, marrying that so called psycho bitch will bring the Harding's and the Gallagher's together. Just try not to have a bloody union."

He chuckles, "I'll leave that to you, Kenna, besides I doubt Melissa would be able to shoot anyone, let alone kill them."

"So, she's carrying your baby."

He closes his eyes, "I know. Shit. This is a clusterfuck if there ever was one."

"Now, why are you really here?"

He grins, "Oh, Granda is coming over next month. He wants to have a meeting with all of the Bosses here. He's wanting to take over the Midwest now too. He's got Liam ready to take over and he wants Hayden as the Underboss of Chicago."

I frown, why on Earth is he wanting that? "I hate not knowing shit."

Danny nods, "Yeah, tell me about it. Anyway, before he gets here, he needs you to tell Granda who you are."

I blink, it takes me a couple of seconds to realize what he's talking about, more like who he's talking about, and I can't stop the laughter that bubbles out. "Oh shit. That's hilarious. Please tell me you're not leaving yet?"

Danny shakes his head, "No, I'm here for the next week."

I grin, "Killian, how long are you here for?"

Killian's eyes narrow but the smile breaks through when he realizes where I'm going with this. "Not sure yet, but I'm there on Sunday."

I nod. "Danny, you're coming with us for dinner on Sunday and please, for the love of God, will you please call him Granda?"

Danny laughs, "Yeah, Kenna, I'll call him Granda."

"Will you call bitch face Granny?"

Killian bursts out laughing. Tears stream down his face as he tries to get himself under control. "Fuck, now that I've got to see."

"You're a bitch you know that?" Danny asks but there's no heat in his words. "But sure, I'll call the wicked witch of the west Granny. Now, I've got shit to do." He opens his arms and I walk into them. I've missed him; out of all my nieces and nephews Danny is the one that I'm closest to. "Don't be a stranger, Makenna, it's been too fucking long," he whispers. I nod in agreement, it's been at least six months since I last saw him. "I had to get my arse on a plane to come and see you."

I laugh, now that I believe. That's the real reason he's here. I love that he wanted to see me. "Sort this shit out, Danny; marry her. If she's as much of a bitch as you say she is, then we'll deal with her when the baby is born," I tell him as I step out of his arms. "But I'd go to Granda first and tell him that you want an alliance with the Harding's, that you believe that marrying Melissa would be the best way to go about it."

"How the hell did you get so smart?"

"I was born that way," I answer with a smirk. "I'd call him now and do it. The last thing you need is for Melissa's condition to get out first."

He nods, "I'm on it, thanks, Kenna."

"Anytime," I reply and he gives me a smile before shaking hands with Dante and giving the stupid man chin lift to both Alessio and Romero.

I turn to Killian, "So, what did you want to see me for?"

He shakes his head, "I was to relay what Danny boy did, so he did it for me, saved you going ballistic on me.

You're always nicer to him for some reason."

I shrug, "Up until today, he hadn't pissed me off."

Killian laughs, "Noted. I must admit, your Italian isn't that bad."

I shake my head, "His name is Dante. Use it."

"Not going to happen just yet, but we'll see."

I sigh, "I'm going. Call if you need me, and please, for the love of all that's holy, keep Danny out of trouble."

"He can't really get into much more, now can he?"

I glare at him, "Oh yes, he can. What if he does it again to someone over here?"

"Fucking idiot," Killian grouses. "I'll keep him out of trouble. Do you need anything?"

"Not right now, but if I do, I'll call," I tell him as I stand beside Dante, his hand immediately rests on my waist. "I need food."

"Well let's get you some. Wouldn't want anyone thinking I'm not taking care of my bride," Dante says as he tightens his hand on my waist and guides me out of the house. I wave goodbye to Killian and climb into the car.

THE JOURNEY IS QUIET, I WAS TRYING TO SEE IF I COULD find another way for Danny but ultimately there isn't. If he doesn't marry Melissa, then a war will break out between the Gallagher's and the Harding's. While I have no issue with that happening if it needed to, I'd rather work it if there's a way to bring the two biggest crime families in the UK together. That's a good thing and I think if the shoe were on the other foot and it wasn't Danny who had fucked up, he'd have agreed with me.

I pull up outside a small mom and pop restaurant. I eat here a lot, it's owned by a friend of mine's family and whenever I'm in town, I always stop by for some food. Dante, Romero, and Alessio follow behind me as I enter the restaurant.

"Mrs Bianchi, it's lovely to see you again," Maddie says and I laugh, she's only calling me that because Dante's here.

"Maddie, how are you?"

Her eyes flash as she takes in the men behind me. "I'm good, how are you? I heard you were shot."

"Someone has a big mouth," I reply knowing damn well that it was one or all of my brothers. "Maddie, this is Dante, my husband, and his brothers Romero and Alessio."

"Nice to meet you gentlemen. Now, please, take a seat and I'll bring you some menus. Can I get you anything to drink while you look over the menu?"

"Usual for me please," I tell her as I slide into the back both.

"I'll have a black coffee," Dante says and sits beside me. After glancing at the menu, he orders a steak dinner. His hand coming to rest on my knee. I don't listen to what the others want, my gaze is focused on my husband. "Are you okay?"

I nod, "Yeah, why wouldn't I be?"

He clicks his tongue against the roof of his mouth. "Just asking. This is new territory for me," he says quietly, making sure that his brothers don't overhear. "Seeing you in the ring was difficult. I wanted to climb in there and smash your fucking nephew in the face."

I smile at his caring words.

"But I was hard as fucking stone as I watched you beat the shit out of him. You drive me insane, Makenna. You're fucking gorgeous, you look demure, like butter wouldn't melt and yet you're probably the most dangerous woman in the world."

I shrug, "And I'm all yours."

His eyes flash at my words and he nips at my lip. "Damn fucking straight you are. Tonight, I'm going to worship your body, baby. I have to give that tattoo of yours some attention."

My breath hitches at his words. "I'm not going to stop you."

Romero and Alessio take their seats opposite us and I turn my attention from my husband to them. I raise my brow when I see them both staring at me expectantly.

"Okay, I've gotta ask..." Alessio begin. "Who is Danny going to call Grandad and Granny?"

I smile, just thinking about him doing it. It's going to be so much fun. I love fucking with my family and having him call my parents that will be perfect. "My Mom and Da. Denis, my brother, is my Da's eldest child. He and Denis' mom were never married. Denis has too many fucking kids. I'm pretty sure his bitch of a wife is pregnant again, making it baby number six. Anyway, Danny is my nephew, which makes my da his granda."

Alessio's lips twitch, "Oh shit, that'll be a fun dinner."

I grin, "Yes, it's going to be hilarious. I'll drop the bombshell first about who I am." Dante's hand covers mine and his thumb starts to caress my skin. "Then, Danny will drop his bomb, which in turn will take the heat away from me and onto Da."

Maddie comes back with our drinks and the conversation stops. Romero has a weird look on his face and I decide that now is the time to address the problem.

"You think I don't like you, don't you?" I ask him and watch as his brows knit together. "Answer me, please?" I ask nicely.

He shrugs like it doesn't matter. "You don't know me."

I roll my eyes at his stupid answer. "Romero, you're right I don't know you, but I certainly don't hate you. In fact, I have a job lined up for you."

Oh, now that gets his interest, although I know he's leery. "What type of job?"

"As you now know, I run the east coast, all except for New York. Which also means that Dante does too and when Dante takes over from your father…" The sooner the fucking better in my opinion. "Then Dante and I will run New York too." I turn to Dante, "Your Granda still the Capo dei Capi?" He nods, "Okay so, when the old man kicks it, Dante will take over. Which will mean he'll be looking for Underbosses."

Romero leans forward in his seat, eager to hear where I'm going with this.

"I need an Underboss for Connecticut. I want you to take the position and when the time comes and Dante becomes Capo dei Capi, I hope that you'll then in turn become the Underboss for the Italian Mafia for New York."

I sit back in my chair as Maddie starts to walk over to us. I've given him my offer now it's up to him to think it through and let me know what he decides.

"Fuck, Kenna." Dante's voice is husky and full of heat. "When I get you home, I'm not letting you up for air. I hope you fill your belly now, it's the only chance you'll get today."

I laugh as Maddie places our plates onto the table in front of us. "If you guys need anything, just yell."

"Thanks, Mad," I tell her as I pick up my knife and fork.

"Anytime, Kenna. Enjoy." She saunters off and I bite my lip as I notice that Alessio watches her ass sway as she walks away.

"What's the catch?" Romero asks and I smile, he's smart as hell. "I'm not stupid, Makenna. I know you wouldn't offer me the position if there wasn't something in it for you."

"Actually there's nothing in it for me," I reply instantly. "The position is yours, you'll have to deal with the ignorance of the Irish men. They will not want an Italian leading them. It's bad enough that I'm married to one." I turn to Dante. "Their words, not mine," I tell him in hopes of softening the blow. "But ultimately, Romero, it's your decision. You could marry an Irish woman. It would give you the respect that not marrying one would have. It would also mean you're part of the family and all the perks that come with it."

He's silent, carefully watching me, so I say what I need to and then leave him be. "Look, I don't care if you hate that I'm the Boss. It doesn't bother me. I haven't offered you this position because you're my husband's brother. If it were that reason, I'd offer Alessio the position too. You have a lot of potential, Romero, and right now, you're standing in the shadows when you really shouldn't be. Dante is going to lead, that was a given, but you? You deserve to forge your own path. I'm giving you that opportunity. As I said, you can go it alone or you can marry a Gallagher. We're not all raving psychopaths. Some of us are more docile than others. The choice is yours; just think about it and let me know."

I start eating, and let what I've just said linger in the air. If Romero is smart he'll take the position and the opportunity to marry into the family. I have the perfect person lined up for him. She's sweet and soft, she'll bring out his protective instincts.

TWELVE

Dante

EVERYONE IS silent as we finish our food. Romero's still in shock, I was surprised that she offered him the position, but it makes sense. I also believe that she has a hidden agenda and when I get home, I'm going to find out what the hell she actually wants.

"Are we going to Makenna's or are we going to ours?" Alessio asks and I don't answer. After spending just a night in Makenna's house, I don't want to go back to my fucking apartment.

"You can stay with me until I find a bigger house," she says not lifting her eyes from her cell. She's been engrossed in whatever the hell is on the screen for the past five minutes.

"Bigger house?" Romero echoes.

She sighs as she taps her phone and places it down onto the table. She finally looks up. "Yes, a bigger house. I may only be married to your brother for a day, but I know that you three share a bond and that means your asses are where we are. So yes, I'm going to find a bigger house, something that all four of us can live in and we won't be ready to kill each other within a few days."

Both of my brothers stare at her, the respect they have for her isn't just because she's the Boss. We've only been married for twenty four hours but she's shown us who she is and how loyal she is. From saving Alessio and not breaking a sweat, to sharing her home with us all, giving Romero a position that means he'll have power and not just as my brother, but now, she wants to get a house where we all can live.

She says she doesn't know how to love but she does, every single thing she's done for us so far has been out of love. Oh, I know that she'd never admit it, hell most of the time she glares at Romero like she wants to kill him, but deep down she cares and for that reason alone, we'll always have her back.

"Kenna, would you like anything else?" the server asks and I see Alessio giving her his panty-dropping smile.

"No, thanks, Mads," Kenna replies with a smile.

The server nods and picks up our empty plates then walks away.

"Owww. What the fuck?" Alessio glares at Makenna who's smiling sweetly at him. "Why the hell did you kick me?"

She raises a brow at his tone, "Keep your eyes to yourself, arsehole. She is not someone you fuck with." Her voice is darker and harder than I have ever heard before.

Alessio glares at her, he's always hated someone telling him who he can and can't fuck.

Makenna reaches for my hand under the table and squeezes. "Listen to me, Alessio. Maddie is my friend, she's not just some random woman you can fuck. She's had enough of arseholes to last her a lifetime. You want a quick screw, go find someone else, I'm sure there's plenty of willing women. Just not her."

The table is silent as we wait for either of them to say something. When Alessio sits back in his chair, I know that he's not going to respond to her. She turns to me, a small smile on her face. "Ready to go?"

I nod and slide out of the booth pulling her with me, her smile widens and she leans into my body. Her softness and curves makes my dick stir, as it does whenever I'm around her. "You okay, baby?"

Her eyes flash with irritation, "Baby?"

Ah so that's what she's pissed about. "What would you like me to call you?" I ask as we leave the restaurant.

"I can name a few," Romero comments. "Psycho is the most obvious one."

Makenna's lips twitch, "It takes one to know one, Romero."

He scoffs, "Please, I'm perfectly normal in comparison."

Both Alessio and I chuckle at their banter, Makenna throws her head back and laughs, "Wrong. I'm well-adjusted to what I am Romero. I don't hide behind the darkness, in fact, I embrace it. It's who I am, who we all are. Let your crazy come out to play sometime." She fucking winks at him leaving him standing there slack-jawed, watching her walk away.

I slap him on the back as Makenna climbs into the car. "What the hell?" he mutters once she closes the door. "How the hell does she know so much about us?"

I walk around to the front of the car, "I have no idea. What I have learned is that she's fucking smart, intuitive, and savvy. I wouldn't be surprised if she's done a whole lot of research before marrying me. After what Dad did to her, I wouldn't put it past her. Know your enemy and all that."

He nods and we climb into the car.

"I did research you. All of you," she says once she pulls into traffic letting me know that she heard our conversation. "But I know more by observing. Romero, you're the quiet one. You've stood in the shadows of your brother for too long."

"Look, Kenna," he says and I know from him calling her by her name, he likes her. Not that I didn't already know, but having him call her Kenna cements that. "I get that you're a badass, but you know nothing about me."

She nods, but her face is void of emotion. "Okay, if you say so."

"Oh, wise one, enlighten me," he quips as he rolls his eyes.

Makenna's lips twitch. "Fine," she spits. "You're the middle child, the one that was overlooked. Your mom, because Alessio was the youngest, meaning she spent more time with him than you. Your father, because he was grooming Dante to take over the empire. You had to find your ground and you did, but not in the way you had thought."

"Keep going," he says, his jaw clenched tight.

"I don't know what happened, but I can guess. How old were you when you killed first?" she asks but she doesn't let him answer. "My guess, you were young, probably not even a teenager. It shaped you, made you believe that you had something inside that needed caging. You may have even been told that."

He nods and I glance at Alessio, he's watching enthralled, but wary, we didn't know this about Romero. "Mom was the first one to find me after I had killed the men."

Makenna sighs, "What did she tell you?"

"That I was a monster, that whatever was inside was evil just like our dad." His words are cold and even though he's hiding it, I can tell that what our mother said stuck with him.

Makenna's grip on the steering wheel tightens. "You are not a monster. We are not monsters. What we do isn't easy. Not everyone could do it. Look I'm not blowing smoke up your ass, you're Dante's brother and I could have left you and not asked you to take over one of my cities, but I have. You can control your emotions, you're able to keep cool despite what's going on around you, and if need be, you're able to kill without hesitation. That's not being a monster."

Silence fills the car. I look at my wife, she's fucking beautiful and she's right. Romero has more potential than what he's been given.

"What is it called then?" Alessio asks.

"It's called being *made*. It's what we do. It's who we are. It's ingrained in us from a young age. Sometimes, people are born with it, like Alessio and Dante. And other times, we're shaped to become them, like Romero and I are. The difference between us and them, is when we cross the line, there's no coming back."

"How far have you gone?" Romero asks and it's as though they're talking another language because I have no idea what the hell they're talking about.

"Further than you. I've killed more men than I can count. Including family."

Romero nods and sits back in his seat, his arms crossed over his chest and closes his eyes. "What do you think would be the best course of action to take over as the Underboss of Connecticut?"

My lips twitch, good, he's finally taking this seriously.

"Are you asking me or Dante?" she asks him as she glances at me looking confused.

"Both of you. I want to know what you both think."

I nod, "I think it's a great move. You should have been made an Underboss already and the fact that you haven't is our father's way of pulling your strings. It's bullshit. Makenna's giving you the opportunity to do what you should have been doing all along. Take it. As for the best course of action—do you see yourself falling in love?"

He laughs. "No, fuck, no. We don't do that shit," he tells me and I catch the hurt that flashes through Makenna's eyes.

"Sometimes it sneaks up on you," I tell him while looking at my wife. I never thought I'd love someone but in the past twenty four hours that thought has vanished. Makenna has gotten under my skin and pierced my dead heart.

"For you to gain respect from the men, I recommend you marry Holly. You met her brother today. It would mean that you're stronger as you're tied to the Gallagher family, giving you their full backing. You'd be the husband of the great-granddaughter of the Mafia. But ultimately Romero, you're going to have to lead these men. Show them that you're not a fucking fool. Show them your dark side and fucking embrace it."

"Have you spoken to your grandfather about this?" he asks and I don't interrupt. It's going to be his position and he only should come to the decision.

If it were anyone else other than Makenna offering him the position over the Irish Mafia I'd have told him fuck no and put a bullet in their head. But it's her and I know that she's only wanting to build her empire, and by doing so, she wants the best of the best defending her.

"Yes, I wouldn't have asked if I hadn't run it past

Granda, he agrees that Holly would be the perfect choice. You being Underboss for me is my decision and mine alone. That wasn't ran past anyone."

He sighs as he scrubs a hand down his face, he's frustrated.

"Romero, you have twenty-four hours to give me an answer. If you decide to marry Holly, Granda will set the engagement up and you'll have a quick wedding. If you don't want to marry Holly and do want to be my Underboss then you'll be introduced at the next meeting we have."

Romero nods, "Thank you."

She ignores his thanks and turns to me. "Are you ready for the shit storm that's about to happen?" I take her hand and hold tight, "Da's going to go mental."

"He'll be fine, once he gets over the shock. Besides, you've already set it up to have Danny turn up. It'll be fine. What can he do?" If he even thinks about hurting her, I'll end him. I don't give a fuck.

She nods, "I spoke to both Danny and Killian about that fucker Kurt and they're both working on it. Killian has enough contacts to find out anything I need and Danny, well that arsehole, is useful in his own way."

"What's up with Danny anyway?" Alessio asks, "You and he are really close."

Makenna's eyes narrow. "Yeah, and?" Her Irish accent is thicker, I've come to learn when she's annoyed or pissed off her accent gets heavier and thicker. Hell when she was talking with Danny and Killian, her accent was thick and fast.

Alessio grins, "I just meant how did you become so close. You're not siblings."

She shrugs, "When I was in Ireland, I stayed in Denis' house. Danny, Malcolm, and Holly are all older than me.

Well Holly is a few months older than me. We're all really close. There's no rivalry as we're all doing what we want to. I run the east coast, Danny runs the UK, Mal runs Spain, and Holly, well that woman makes sure that our money is safe. She has a legitimate business and makes investments for all of us. If you were to marry her, she'd set up a business over here."

She glances in the rear-view mirror and whatever she sees makes her sigh. "I'm not a bitch to everyone. Especially not my family unless they warrant it. I don't like people, I fucking hate most of them and I'm a woman ruling a man's world. Those men that are below me constantly try to test me, hence why my Granda thought marriage would help. He was sick of me killing my men."

I know that it makes sense having us married but hearing her detail why pisses me off.

"Any more questions?"

"Yeah, just how old is your brother?" Romero asks with a grin.

"Denis is forty, Fin is thirty three, Patrick is twenty nine, and Cian is twenty-five. Denis' children are: Danny, twenty-two, Malcolm, twenty-one and, Holly is twenty. Then there's a break, and the next range from thirteen to six months."

"Jesus," Romero mutters.

"Yep, tell me about it. Now Danny's starting." She shakes her head, but not in disgust, she looks disappointed.

"Romero and Alessio, are you coming home with us or do you need me to drop you off somewhere?" She squeezes my hand and I watch the heat spread through her cheeks.

"Drop them off at our apartment, they can come back later this evening," I tell them and she smiles at me. "I want you to find out who the fuck Kurt works for," I instruct my brothers.

They nod, "I'll talk to our father. See what he has to say, you know what he's like, if I make out that Makenna's being a bitch it'll loosen his lips," Romero tells me and I caress Makenna's hand with my thumb.

"When we find out who is behind it, we're going to end them all," Alessio tells us.

"It would be the perfect way to get rid of your father," Makenna says softly. "Pretend that Kurt killed him, that your father found out that Kurt was behind the hit at the wedding. After all, Alessio was shot, your father was outraged and confronted Kurt when he discovered the betrayal. Kurt, who is already fucked, did what any man who's fighting for their life does. He shoots your father and kills him. Then, you take out Kurt for not only shooting Alessio and I, but also killing your father. You had to put him down. Case closed, everyone mourns that fucking arshole, no one knows that you killed him and you get to become Capo." She gives me a bright smile, she's a fucking genius.

"Holy shit that could actually work," Alessio grunts.

Makenna's lips turn up in disgust, "Of course it will work," she sneers, probably pissed that he was shocked that she came up with it.

"It's fucking brilliant and it's what we'll do. No one is going to see it coming. We're all going to be focused on finding out what the hell happened at the wedding and getting revenge on the Bratva. Nobody is going to be looking at us and our father," I tell her and I'm rewarded as she smiles at me, her eyes full of brightness.

Makenna pulls up out front of our apartment building. "Are you going with them?" There's a slight hesitancy in her voice, I fucking hate it.

"No, I'm staying with you. Always." The relief in her eyes would bring a better man down. "Romero will grab the bag I have packed."

"Okay," she says softly.

"Makenna?" Romero says as he's getting out of the car. She turns to look at him and I do the same. "Set up the wedding." He closes the car door behind him and walks toward the apartment.

"You knew he'd say yes, didn't you?" I ask her as she drives off.

"Yes, what Romero doesn't know is that my Granda is hell bent on taking over the entire USA, he wants every state to be run by the Irish. Holly is Irish, she's a woman who wasn't trained as I was, but her husband and any husband of the women born a Gallagher will take over as Underboss. But Romero has skills that could see him as Boss. Skills that would put him ahead of any of the other married *made men*."

Holy fuck, Romero would fucking love that. It's something he would never have thought off.

"Dante, you'll be Boss soon enough. Have you thought about doing the same as my Granda has?"

"Taking over more than the east coast?" She nods. "No, I haven't, but I'm also not going to dismiss the idea either."

"You want to take over the world, I'd stand by your side and take everyone down as you do," she tells me with a soft smile.

Fuck. Hearing those words makes my chest burn. "When I get you home, I'm going to fuck you, Kenna."

Her breathing deepens as her cheeks flush. "Dante."

I grin, "Yeah, baby, that's what you're going to say when you scream out your release."

She sighs as she squirms in her seat. Less than five minutes and I'll be inside of her. "Fuck," she whimpers.

"Oh, baby, that's exactly what we're going to do."

She glares at me but I can't keep the smirk from my face. I'm going to worship every inch of her body, paying close attention to the Gallagher crest tattoo she has on her ass.

THIRTEEN

Makenna

I TAKE a deep breath as I open the front door to my parent's house. Romero and Alessio are a step behind Dante and I. I'm actually nervous about what's going to happen today, but there's not much that I can do. I'm here an hour before Killian and Danny are due to arrive as I need to talk to my da in private.

Things between Dante and I are amazing. Our relationship has gotten stronger and stronger. . It's been three days since I met with Killian and Danny, four days since Dante and I have been married and yet it feels like years. We're getting closer and I can feel myself falling for him. It's stupid, but I can't help it. If he betrays me, it'll destroy me and I'll kill him.

"Hello? Anyone home?" I call out as I step into the hall and Alessio closes the door behind him.

"Nope," Finn replies and I smile. "You're early, Ma's panicking."

I roll my eyes, "I'm early 'cause I need to talk to Da, where is he?"

"What? Am I not good enough?" Finn grins at me and

this is why I return every Sunday. Things between us Gallagher children are easy and we all love each other.

"Shut it," Da tells him as he steps into the hall. "She wants her da." He pulls me into his arms, obviously not giving a shit that the Bianchi's are here.

"Do you have some time? I need to talk to you," I ask as I nibble on my bottom lip. I hate feeling this way, I'm not usually like this, but I hate the thought of my da being disappointed in me. I'm still his little girl, hell I always will be.

"For you, always." He leads me toward his office.

Dante, Romero, Alessio are behind us. Dante made it clear that he'd be with me when talking to my da, I think he believes that my da will hurt me when he finds out the truth.

Once we're in the office, Da takes a seat and I take one opposite. The door closes and I turn to see not only are Dante and his brothers here, but mine are also. Great, just what I need, an audience.

"What's going on Makenna?" Da's voice is hard, he's not usually like this with me, but I see the worry in his eyes.

"You're not going to like what I'm about to tell you and I'm sorry for that."

His nostrils flare and his eyes flash with warning. "Start talking," he demands as he sits back in his chair and glares at Dante.

"After what happened to me, Killian thought it would be best to train me. He didn't want me to be vulnerable…"

"He did what?" Dad grinds out, his jaw clenched.

"Da…" I tell him giving him a look, he sighs and waves for me to continue. "Anyway, when Killian thought I was trained enough, he took me to Ireland. Granda decided that Killian had done a great job that I'd be best served coming back here and taking over the business."

Da gets to his feet, his palms slamming down on the table as his chair topples over. "Over my fucking dead body!" he roars, his torso leaning forward as he glares at me.

I get to my feet. "Too late, Da. I've been running the east coast since I was seventeen. I know you don't like it, but there's nothing you can do about it. You rule New York, I rule the rest of the east coast. I wouldn't have told you except Granda is coming over next month and wants a meeting with everyone."

Da lets out a low growl. "Kenna…" he says and my heart hurts for him, he sounds tortured. "This life, it's…"

"I know, Da," I say interrupting him. "I know first-hand what it is, I've been on both ends of this world and I'm here standing. Don't make me out to be this perfect little girl. I'm far from it."

He sighs, his jaw clenches and he rights his chair. "I didn't want this for you," he tells me as he sits down. "But from everything I've heard from my men, the Boss of the east coast is a fucking monster."

I smirk at his words. Yeah, I'm the bitch, I'll make my men pay if they fuck up and if anyone tries to hurt the family, they won't get the chance to live to regret it.

"You can't be serious?" Finn snaps and this is why I wanted it to be just Da, my brothers are over emotional when it comes to me. Finn especially as he was the one that found me lying in a pool of blood. "Da, what the fuck?"

Da shakes his head, "I don't like this, not one bit."

I get to my feet again, Dante's hand is on my hip instantly and I love that he's right here with me. "I'm sorry, but that's something you're going to have to take up with Granda."

"So you're really the Boss of the east coast?" Cian asks with a grin.

I roll my eyes, "What do you want?"

He throws his head back and laughs, "Always so distrusting."

I flip him the bird and turn my attention back to my da. "I know you're pissed, but there's nothing we can do about it now. You sent me away. Killian did what he thought was best and then Granda took over."

"I'll talk to your Grandfather about this."

I shrug, "You do that, it's not going to change anything, Da. Just the same way it's not going to change that Denis rules Ireland. Or that Granda is wanting to take over the mid-west and wants Liam to rule that and wants Hayden to be Underboss of Chicago."

His eyes widen a fraction before he composes himself and then he slowly nods. "Okay, I take it your husband knows about this?"

I roll my eyes, "Of course he does, Da."

"Wait, who's Denis?" Patrick questions looking between Da and I.

We both ignore him. "Look, Da, I get it, you're pissed. But nothing is going to change what's happened, what I am. You need to deal with it and then we can move on to more pressing matters."

Just like that, my da changes, gone is the pissed off father, in his place is the Boss. "What's happened?"

I sigh, thank God, he's moved on from that. "We found out that the ambush at our wedding was actually a betrayal. One of the henchmen for the Famiglia hit the deck before the shooting even started. We need to find out who he's working for and then take them down."

"We?" Patrick echoes and I glare at him. "Makenna, you can't be serious."

I lift my boot and slide my hand in, my fingers connecting with the handle of my knife. In one swift move,

I lift the knife from my boot and throw it across the room. It pierces Patrick's shirt, just above his shoulder and embeds both his shirt and the tip of the knife in the wall. "Next time you question me, I will go for your throat."

My brothers all stare at me as though they've never seen me before. I ignore them and focus on my da, who's grinning like a lunatic. "We'll figure out who the fuck is betraying Dante, then we'll deal with it. You may be a Bianchi, son, but you're now a Gallagher too. We take care of our own."

The doorbell sounds and Da frowns, he has no idea what's about to happen. Glancing at my watch I see that Killian and Danny are fifteen minutes early.

"Um, Da..." I say but it's too late, the office door opens and in strolls my uncle and nephew.

"Seamus," Killian says with a grin.

Danny has a grin on his face and I bite the inside of my lip to stop myself from smiling. "Granda," Danny says with a nod of the head.

Da's face is slack as he takes in Danny. Anyone with a fucking brain can see that Danny's related to us, he's the image of Denis, who looks like Da.

"Da, this is Denis' son, Danny," I say making the introductions.

"Fuck," Killian comments as he stares at my da.

"Get over here," Da grunts to Danny and I watch on as he walks over to my father and gets pulled into a hug. "Fuck, it's good to see you."

When my da releases him, Danny walks over to me and throws his arm over my shoulder. "You okay?" he asks and I nod. "You tell him?"

"Yeah, Danny, I told him. What about you, you get that thing sorted?"

He grins, "Yep, I called Da and told him, then I called

Melissa. She's pissed to say the least but we're getting married. I've to deal with that arsehole of a brother of hers when I get back. But you were right."

Killian groans, "Don't fucking tell her that."

I laugh, "I always am."

Danny rolls his eyes, "And so modest too."

"What the hell are we missing?" Finn asks and I turn to Da and see him staring at Danny and me.

Taking a deep breath I steady myself to tell them the story. "When I went to Ireland, I was shocked. When Da was seventeen, he fell in love. This woman was the love of his life and if Da had the choice, she'd have been the woman that he married but he was already engaged to our mother. Anyway, this woman got pregnant and because she was unwed and only seventeen, she was sent to a home where pregnant women go."

I turn to Danny and see he's looking down at me with a smile on his face. Glancing back at Da, I find him with his head bowed as he sits in his chair. "Da was forced to marry Mom, even though he didn't want to. Granda had already promised her parents they'd be married and well we all know what happens when you renege on a promise." I turn to my brothers and find them starting at me, their attention on me as they wait for me to finish the story.

"So when the woman came home, she had a baby with her. Denis. By this time, Mom had demanded that Da leave Ireland and to come here where they started a new life. Mom didn't want Denis to be a part of our lives and Da agreed."

"What the fuck?" Cian growls as he glares at Da.

"Yeah, so we have a brother. He's forty. He's the one that rules Ireland, and he's cool as fuck. This is his eldest son, Danny, he also has five other children. Malcolm rules Spain and I'm pretty sure Holly will be moving here soon,"

I inform them, knowing that Da has no idea about any of this. Or so I thought, but looking at him now and remembering his interaction with Danny, I realize I was wrong. Da knew about Dan. But how?

"Denis and I have been in contact recently, he's told me all about his family, although he did leave out that he's met you," Da explains, probably seeing the confusion on my face.

I nod, "Danny, these are my brothers. Finn, Patrick, and Cian. Guys, this is your nephew, Danny."

Danny removes his arm from my shoulder and I take a step backward into Dante's arms. He kisses the top of my head and I shiver at his touch.

"It's nice to finally meet you," Danny says as he shakes their hands.

"Same," Cian replies with a smile that helps me relax; things between them are going to be fine.

There's a knock on the office door and I know it's' Ma. "Dinner is ready," she tells us, not coming in. She's not allowed, this is Da's space.

"Coming," Da replies and starts shooing us out of the room.

Once we're in the dining room we all take a seat. Ma has the servers bring out the food. Everyone's silent, probably trying to wrap their heads around what they've just found out.

"This is fantastic," Danny says taking another bite of food. "Thanks Granny."

I bite my lip to stop the laughter from bubbling out. Killian chuckles and my brothers are trying their best to hide their laughter.

Ma gasps as her hand comes up to rest on her chest. I roll my eyes at her dramatics.

"Oh, Danny, you should tell them your news," I say

with the biggest grin on my face and Killian's chuckle turns into full laughter.

Danny's eyes widen and he grins. "Oh yeah, so, I'm getting married and Melissa's pregnant. You're going to be a great granda and great granny."

Ma's gasp is even more audible and Da stares at us like we're crazy.

"Da, he's being serious. You're going to be a great-granda."

He smiles brightly and that has the rest of us laughing. Finn, Patrick, and Cian can't hold their laughter back, Cian's wiping his eyes where the tears are.

"God, this is hilarious. So, Ma, you ready to be a great granny?"

"What the hell? Will someone please tell me what's going on?" Ma demands as she glances around the table.

"You may remember my granny? Lisa Morland."

I've never seen my ma look so pale in my life. "What the hell are you doing here?" she demands.

"I invited him. After all, he is my nephew. If anyone shouldn't be here, it's you."

She snarls at me, "Don't be a bitch."

I laugh, "Really, Ma? You really want to go there?"

"Makenna, I don't think this is the time," Killian tells me and I realize he knows what's happened.

"Someone had better tell me what the hell is going on," Da says looking between mom and I.

"Nothing, Seamus," Ma says as she goes back to eating.

"It's obviously not nothing. Fucking answer me," he demands, his hand slamming down onto the table making her jump.

"What I really want to know," Finn begins, "is why Makenna hates you."

I sigh, this isn't what we should be discussing. I was

pissed that she was being a bitch to Danny.

"Leave it alone, Finn, this has nothing to do with you," Ma says softly, trying her hardest to move the conversation onto something else. "So, Danny, what do you do?"

Danny glares at her. "Fuck you."

"Oh Jesus," Killian mutters. "Danny boy, did you really have to say that?"

Danny nods, "Yes, she's a fucking cunt and while I know why Makenna never said anything, I don't understand it. If it were me, I'd have gutted her where she stood."

"Danny," I warn, he's pushing this now and it's not the bloody time.

"Holy fuck!" Finn growls, "It was you?"

"Finn, not now," Killian warns.

"What's going on, Killian?" I ask, he's not wanting this to blow up. I get it, I know what's going to happen but this is Killian, the man kills for fun.

He sighs, "Your Granda wants to sort her out." Ma gasps as tears spring to her eyes. "But that's not going to happen now. Fucking hell. I shouldn't have worn my good shoes."

"What the hell am I missing?" Da asks, glaring around the table.

To my surprise it's Dante that answers him. "What the other's know that you don't is who it was that slit Makenna's throat."

Da's eyes flash. "Tell me now," he grinds out and I've never seen him so angry. His hands are shaking, his nostrils are flaring and he looks as though he's going to cry.

"Tell me."

"It was Ma," Finn says and the room is filled with silence. You can hear a pin drop.

"It was you?" Da growls as he gets to his feet. "You're

the one that tried to kill my daughter?"

"Seamus, I'm sorry, it was a mistake," Ma says as she gets to her feet, trying to worm her way out of it.

I throw my fork onto the table and sit back in my chair. There's no way I'm eating after this shit.

"Mistake? Tell me what the fuck happened!" he tells her as he advances on her. "Start talking, now," he demands as he boxes her in.

"I was having an affair," she tells him softly, but Da doesn't give a fuck about that right now. "Makenna found out and he was mad. He hurt her and demanded that I finish her off. If I didn't, then he was going to tell you and he'd have killed her."

"So you slit her fucking throat? That is your daughter. You should have come to me, I would have protected her," Da yells as the tears stream down Ma's face. "Who was it? Hmm, who meant more to you than our daughter?"

Ma doesn't answer him and Da loses his patience, he puts his fist into the wall behind her causing her to squeal.

"Someone tell me who the fucking bastard was?" Da demands and my heart sinks. This is why I never said anything, my da is beyond angry. I know there's no coming back from this.

"It was my father," Dante tells him and Da loses it.

He pulls out his knife from his pant leg and slices it across ma's throat, slitting it from ear to ear. The shock on Ma's face as she realizes what's happened is karma. She doesn't make a sound as she falls to the floor in a heap, her eyes wide open as Da turns to face us. His eyes are wild; anger, pain, disgust, and worry feature heavily in them.

I turn to Finn, he's panting, his fist clenched and jaw tight as he stares down at our mother's dead body. He's not able to take his eyes off her. Looking at Patrick, I see his gaze on the floor, his brows pinched and I see a tear fall down his face. Out of all of us, he was the one that was closest to her. My attention turns to Cian, he is very much like Finn, his chest heaving as he stares widely at the scene in front of him.

I'm numb but relief washes over me. She's no longer going to have the opportunity to hurt me again. I should feel something—guilt, anger, pain. But I don't, I feel bad that my brothers are hurting, that my da's hurting, but I'm not. I'm glad the bitch is dead.

"Your father isn't going to know what hit him," my da says.

Dante nods, "I already have a plan in place."

Da grins. "Good, I want in. No one hurts my daughter and gets away with it."

I'm pretty sure there was a threat in there somewhere.

"We're the motherfucking Gallagher's," Da says. "We're the ones that strike fear into everyone when they hear our name. We don't keep secrets and we certainly don't fucking keep secrets when it concerns my daughter."

Killian shrugs, "Kenna didn't want you to know and I was never around. I let it be, your boys loved their ma."

"I don't give a fuck. That woman should have paid the consequences a long fucking time ago." Da stomps over to his chair and sits down, picking up his whiskey glass as he does.

"No more secrets, no more lies," he tells us. "We're a family, stronger than ever. We're going to fucking rule the world, that includes being as one with the Italians. To new beginnings and being the motherfucking monsters we were born to be."

We all raise our glasses as we toast. I glance back at my ma who's still on the floor with her eyes open and for the first time since I was twelve I feel a little relief, and yet I know the worst is yet to come.

FOURTEEN

Dante

IT'S BEEN three days since Makenna's father found out the truth about what happened to his daughter and did what any father would do. Killed the bitch that hurt her. Seamus has so many cops on his payroll that he managed to have her death swept under the rug. No one is going to go down for it. It's the way it is in the Mafia. If we know the right people, have them on our payroll, everything can go away. The more money you have the better your life is. It's a fact.

Today, we're going to the funeral. It's a fucking farce and if I had the choice, I'd burn the bitch's body and leave it as that. But Seamus and Makenna both agreed for the sake of Finn, Patrick, and Cian they'd hold a service for her. Since Makenna has to be in attendance, I will be as well.

"Babe," I say as she steps into the bedroom. She's wearing black matching underwear, it's lacy and she looks sexy as fuck.

She turns to glare at me before pulling on her black heels. "Dante, don't. You've already fucked me twice this morning. We have to get ready otherwise we're going to be late."

"I don't give a fuck. Kenna, after everything that bitch did to you, how the hell are you even calm?"

She walks over to me and my dick twitches. Seeing her in just her underwear and heels makes me want to throw her onto the bed and fuck her into complete oblivion. Her hand rests on my chest and she takes a deep breath. I'm completely gone for this woman, there's no if, buts, or maybes. Makenna Bianchi owns me heart and soul. Her other hand rests on my jaw. "Are you going to be by my side?"

"Of course," I scoff. Did she think I wouldn't be?

"That's why I'm calm. Fuck, Dante. We've been together for a week. A fucking week and it feels as though we've been together for a lifetime. Whatever the hell it is between us is real."

"It is, real, raw, and fucking passionate. You're it for me, Makenna," I tell her honestly and watch as she closes her eyes. I rest my forehead against hers. "I'm serious, I'm not going to lose you, Makenna. I'm going to spend the rest of our lives showing you just how much you mean to me."

"You've accepted me from the get go. You never dismissed me and for that alone I do trust you. You want to care for me, protect me, cherish me…"

"Love you," I tell her and her eyes flare with wariness and fear, but also with hope. "Yeah, babe, I fucking love you."

She shakes her head, "It's too soon."

I grip her face between my hands. "Fuck too soon. It's not. I'd die for you. When I met you I knew you were different. Seeing you in that fucking bar, I was drawn to you and I didn't know why. Since then all you have shown me is how loyal, faithful, and fucking amazing you are. There was no way that I couldn't love you."

She looks up at me and I see the vulnerability shine through her. She looks beautiful. "I love you too," she whispers. And that right there is why I'd give my life for this woman. She doesn't bullshit me. She's open and honest, just lets me know whatever she's thinking. No games. Not with me.

I crash my lips against hers and she melts into me. "I'm your husband, I'm also the man that loves you. It's ingrained in me to protect you, but I also know that you're the Boss."

She smiles brightly at me, her eyes light up as she does, she's fucking gorgeous. "We're the Boss," she corrects me.

"We're the Boss and I'd never do anything to undermine you, just as you wouldn't with me. I'm not going to hurt you or betray you. What I want is for us to build a life together." My hands slide down her body to her ass and I pull her flush against my erection.

"Talking about building a life together, is there something you want to tell me?" She has a smile on her face. I don't think I've seen her this carefree before.

I nip at her lip and her hips push against me. "What are you talking about babe?"

She moans when I bite her neck gently. "I'm not on birth control and you've not once used a condom. Are you trying to get me pregnant?"

My body tightens at her words. I realize that she's right, we've not once used any form of contraception. "Are you opposed to children?" I ask cautiously, feeling like an asshole. I should have realized this.

"I'm not opposed. Don't worry about it, if it happens it happens."

I relax, "Good, because there's no way I'm wearing a condom. Nothing gets in between us. Ever."

She grins at me. "A little caveman-ish, don't you think?"

I chuckle, "You're my wife, Makenna, that means you're mine."

She rolls her eyes. "You're a Neanderthal. I've got to get dressed." She raises up onto her toes and kisses my lips gently. "Love you," she whispers and I deepen the kiss.

She pulls away and I can see the reluctance in her eyes. "I need to get ready. Please, will you go see if your brother has found anything out yet?"

I reach for my suit jacket, giving her one last kiss before I leave our bedroom.

"How is she?" Romero asks as I walk into the sitting room. He's sitting on the sofa with a glass of whiskey in his hand.

"As well as can be expected."

He narrows his eyes at me. "What happened? You look…"

"Lighter," Alessio comments from the armchair, he too has a glass of whiskey in his hand.

I ignore them both. "You finally admitted you love her, huh?" Romero comments.

"Jealous that no one loves you?" Makenna says as she waltzes into the room.

Alessio glares at her. "I need to put a damn bell on you."

I smirk, I like that she and my brothers get along. "Romero, my Granda's in town, he wants to talk to you about your marriage to Holly."

Romero sits up straighter. "What does he want?"

Makenna shrugs. "I have no idea. He doesn't know

what my plans are for you, all he knows is that you're agreeable to the union with Holly."

Romero nods and takes a sip of his drink.

"Have you looked her up yet?" I ask and see Makenna smirk, she's not told me anything about the woman she's setting my brother up with. All I know is that she's her niece.

"Not yet. Why?"

Alessio laughs. "In case she's fucking ugly. Knowing your luck, you'd get stuck with the runt of the family."

"You mean like you are?" Makenna fires back and Romero throws his head back and laughs, it's one thing I've learned about her she's fiercely protective of her family. She scrolls through her cell phone and hands it to Romero. "All you had to do was ask. The redhead is Holly."

I watch Romero's reaction carefully, he's good at hiding it but I see the shock along with the sharp intake of breath. He hands Makenna back her phone and she in turn shows me the image. There are three young girls in the picture, along with Makenna and Holly, the other girl looks similar to Holly and must be her sister. She's cute if you like the red hair and freckles, she's also innocent, you can see it written all over her. That's something that Romero would like, he likes his women docile and compliant.

"Romero, did you find out anything?" I ask him as Makenna reaches for her purse.

He shakes his head. "Not yet, it's fucking driving me insane. I'm fucking pissed off that someone has managed to get one over on us."

"We get this funeral over and done with, then we're going to find out who the fuck tried to take us out. Once we do, we're going to make them see what happens when you fuck with a Gallagher or a Bianchi."

I smirk, my wife is bloodthirsty. "It's time to go," I tell her and she nods, I underestimate her constantly. When I think she's going to crumble she doesn't; instead, she grows stronger.

Three hours later, we're sitting in Seamus' sitting room drinking whiskey. Seamus, Killian, Finn, Patrick, Cian, Danny, Romero, Alessio, Makenna, and I are discussing what's going to happen next. Seamus is hell bent on going after my father even though we have a plan in place to ensure that the bastard dies.

"Fucker actually had the balls to shake my hand," Seamus spits out and shakes his head in disgust.

My father was at the funeral and the smirk the fucker had on his face made every single one of us want to kill the motherfucking bastard.

Makenna's on her laptop, she's changed out of her dress and is wearing yoga pants, a tank top, and barefoot. Her hair piled on top of her head in a messy bun, her feet underneath her as she focuses on whatever the fuck she's looking for. She's been doing this every single night, her eyes glued to the laptop. She's not told me what she's searching for but I'm pretty sure she's trying to find out who the fucking traitor is.

I'm sitting beside her, my arm outstretched behind her back. Every now and then, she'll lean back against it, just for a couple of seconds before lifting off. Romero and Alessio think I'm whipped but I don't give a fuck; with Makenna everything is different.

"Fucking, bastard," she snaps as she types away on the keyboard.

"What, babe?" I ask as I look down on her screen and

see Kurt having a meeting with my father.

"I've looked through both Kurt's and your father's finances. Kurt received a twenty-five thousand dollar deposit from an offshore account on the day of our wedding. I've traced that account back to your father."

The silence around the room is deafening as Makenna's words sink in. Blood rushes to my brain and I try to fight back the rage that's burning deep inside. My father paid to have my wife killed, he almost had his son killed.

"Sit the fuck down now. All of you," Makenna snaps. It's then that I realize that I was moving. Not only me, but her father, Finn, and Danny were too. "Today isn't the day we kill him. He's going to be waiting for us and we're going to ensure that he won't be expecting it when it comes. That fucking bastard has taken enough from all of us and now it stops. We're going to make sure that when the time comes, and it's coming, that when that motherfucker dies, Dante's in the position to take over."

Danny sighs, "Why the hell are you so level-headed?"

"Sit down," she tells us again. "We need to come up with a plan. That arsehole is going down and we need to make sure that the plan is meticulous."

"That's why you're the fucking best," a deep voice calls out from the behind us. I turn to see Makenna's grandfather standing in the doorway with a scowl on his face. He's just an older version of Seamus, he has a full head of gray hair and his bright-blue eyes are full of life and darkness.

"Dad, what are you doing here?" Seamus asks as he takes his seat again, the only ones that are still standing are Finn and I.

"I'm here to end that fucking arsehole's reign. He hurt my favorite granddaughter and for that he's going to pay."

"Granda," Makenna chastises him. "Where's Holly?"

"She's at the hotel with her father and Malcolm. I

didn't think it would be right to bring them all here." He gives Seamus a pointed look.

"Wait, who's here?" Cian asks with a frown.

"Danny's brother and sister are here," Makenna informs him. "As is his father." She can't keep the smile off of her face, I know how much her family means to her. She'd do anything to protect them and she's missed them. She's not seen them in six months, although she does speak to them a lot.

"Denis and Malcolm will want in on this conversation. I'm here as a courtesy call. Seamus, if you want them here, they can be here in thirty minutes. If not, we're moving this meeting to the hotel." The old man turns to me. "We've not been introduced, I'm Henry," he tells me as he holds out his hand. I don't hesitate, I reach out and we shake.

"It's good to see you," I tell him, and it's the truth. He may give me some insight into the way Makenna is.

He nods, "And you too, son, you too." He then turns his attention to Romero, "You must be Romero." The two of them shake hands, "You'll do nicely for my Holly. I'm sure you're anxious to meet her."

"Whoa, what the fuck?" Danny grouses.

"Danny boy, stay out of this. This doesn't concern you," Henry says with a bite to his tone.

"The hell it doesn't, that's my fucking sister." Danny's glaring at Romero. "She's not being given to that arsehole."

Henry sighs, "You had no problem when it was Makenna that was forced into a marriage. Besides, I, unlike you, have spoken to Holly and she's agreed to the union. You don't have a say in what's happening. You have your own marriage to worry about."

Danny's eyes flash with anger, "My…"

"Leave it alone, Dan," Makenna tells him, not even looking at him, her gaze on her laptop. "I've spoken to Holly, she's fine."

The fight leaves him and he nods. "Okay, fine, what are we going to do about that Italian arsehole?"

My teeth clench at his words. "Watch it."

He smirks, "Dante, I no longer class you as Italian, you're family."

"Enough," Henry growls. "Seamus, do you have a fucking problem having your son and his family here?"

Seamus sighs as he glances at his sons.

"No he doesn't. This is bullshit." Kenna's pissed off tone cuts through the tension in the room. "I am not going to divide my time between my family. I have done it enough and it has to stop. Next week it's a meeting of the family. Every Boss, Underboss, and *made man* will be in attendance. That means we're all going to be there. The last thing we need is for our men to think there's a fraction in the family." She lifts her head and glares at her brothers then toward her father. "You have a problem with Denis or any of his kids, get the fuck over it. You are not the injured party here. If you treat my nieces and nephews with anything but respect, we're going to have a problem."

Danny grins, "Aww, I feel the love."

"Shut it," Makenna clips but there's a smile on her face. "Okay, Granda, call Denis and tell him to come over. Holly can work in the other dining room and we'll figure out a plan to get rid of Matteo Bianchi once and for all."

My pride for my wife rises; she's fucking magnificent. She always has a level head and manages to not let emotions sway her. Anyone else, they'd have tried to kill my father long before now. But not Kenna. No, she's biding her time, making sure that when she does strike, he's going down and not coming back up.

FIFTEEN

Makenna
───────────

"WHY IS it that both of his children are fucking Bosses and we're not even Underbosses?" Patrick growls looking pissed off. He crosses his arms over his chest as he glares at Granda.

"Seriously?" I sigh, I'm sick of the childish bullshit.

Patrick shrugs, "Yeah, seriously, Kenna. This is what we've worked hard for, every fucking day of our lives and we're still just grunts, yet you and them are Bosses!"

"Did you ever think that maybe, just maybe, it has to do with your father not me?" Granda tells him and I see the anger flash through his eyes.

"You?" He accuses, "Why?"

Da glares at him. "Are you fucking questioning me? None of you have shown anything that proves that you should be moved up the ranks."

I sigh, nothing good comes from conversations like this. This is something that I want nothing to do with. I believe that all of my brother's should have been made Underbosses already, maybe even Bosses but they haven't been close enough to know how things work. They don't have the confidence of our men.

"Don't you see? When the men find out that Makenna is a fucking Boss they're going to think we're chumps," Cian sighs. I clench my teeth. I didn't think Cian would have a problem with who or what I am.

"The men already know. The only people that didn't were your father and you," Granda tells them with a smile. I notice the pissed off looks on all my brothers faces.

Great, just what I need, them to be even more pissed off.

Cian grunts. "Great, just fucking great. Good ol' princess. Gets whatever the fuck she wants."

My heart pounds against my chest at his words. Hurt, unlike anything I've felt before hits me.

"Cian…" Da growls in warning.

"No, Da, fuck that. He's right. Whatever she wants she gets," Patrick replies glaring at me.

I get to my feet, anger and hurt running through my veins. "I get whatever I want?" My voice is thick with anger. "I was the one that was left here while our mother fucked Matteo. I was the one that was beaten by him and then had no energy in my body left to fight as she slit my throat. No one was here to help me."

Everyone in the room has gone deathly quiet, Da and Finn's faces are slack and pale. Patrick and Cian are looking at me as though they've never seen me before. I don't care, I have loved my family, would do anything for them and this is how I'm treated.

"Then I was sent away." I let out a bitter laugh. "You got to live here and live your life to the fullest, never having to worry about when that fucking bitch would strike again." My mouth feels dry as I say the words, I've never admitted to anyone just how scared I was that my mom would try to do it again.

"Kenna..." Da says, his voice tortured.

I ignore him and carry on. "No one was ever here for me. I have always been alone. Always. When I was six and broke my arm when I fell off my bike, not one of you arseholes tried to help me. Instead you laughed and ran off. No one was there when I broke my hand while Killian trained me. No one was there when Granda told me that I was going to be Boss and the men went crazy. No one has ever given a shit. So tell me, arseholes, why should I give a fuck about what you want? Hmm? After all, I get whatever the hell I want. The only fucking thing I ever wanted when I was younger was a family that gave a fuck. Yet, here I am."

I turn to Granda and he's looking at me with a smile on his face and pride in his eyes. "I need a drink. When Denis gets here, I'll be fine."

"Kenna, don't go just yet. I want to talk to you," Da says and I glance at him, he's got tears in his eyes. "I'm so fucking sorry, I failed you."

I don't reply, I've no idea what to even say. Yes, he failed me. Da loves me, that I'm sure of, but I also know that my brothers have always come first.

"I never realized you felt that way, you should have told me."

I scoff, "When, Da? When did I have time? When I came out of the hospital? Oh, yeah, you had me sent off to Killian. By the time I came home I was able to stand on my own two feet and didn't need your help." I'm being bitchy right now and I can't help it. Everything I've felt and bottled up is spilling out of me.

I need Dante.

If someone had told me weeks ago that I'd need

someone in my life I'd have laughed in their face, but right now, I need my husband.

"Makenna, fuck," Finn growls. "I don't give a shit if you're the Boss. Hell, I'd fucking stand beside you and happily do so. I'd protect you until my dying breath. I hated that you were sent away. I fucking demanded you to be here with us where we could protect you. I held you in my arms, held your throat as you bled out." He slams his hand down on Da's desk. "Don't fucking tell me that I don't care. I fucking do and I always have." His face is bright red and his chest is heaving. I've never seen him look so devastated before. "I'd do anything in my power to protect you, Kenna. Everything you've just spewed is bullshit."

"Really?" I can't help the sneer that comes out of my mouth. "What about those two? You really believe they give a shit about me?"

He nods and I step closer to him, he instantly pulls me into his arms. "They don't care about me. I'm the reason ma's dead," I tell him quietly and his arms convulse around me, tightening as it does. "I've got what they've desperately wanted for their entire lives. They hate me."

I feel like that twelve-year-old girl that was lying on the floor bleeding out. Vulnerable.

"I don't give a shit," he growls in my ear. "You've been through so much and came out fighting. You'll always have my love and loyalty, Kenna, always," he tells me and I sink further into his embrace. "If they don't see that, then they're fucking idiots."

I pull back and I'm instantly pulled into Da's arms. "I'm so fucking sorry, Kenna, I should have protected you and I didn't."

I take a deep breath and nod. "It's okay, Da, you did

what you thought was right. I've forgiven you. I did a long time ago."

He sucks in a deep breath and his entire body shudders. "Love you, baby girl. Always have and always will. I'm sorry that you felt that you were alone."

"It's okay, Da. I'm just being bitchy. I don't like being put into a corner. I tend to get my back up."

He chuckles, "Yeah, I know that feeling. Your brothers are being bastards, they're jealous and when they fucking see that they'll realize just how much they've fucked up."

I pull out of his arms and look up into his eyes. The pain in them is so much that it takes everything I have not to look away. "They're hurting right now, Ma's dead, and they're feeling it. I get that. They blame me; I'm the only one they can blame."

"You quite finished?" Granda asks and I nod. "Good. Finn, Patrick, and Cian leave us. We've business to discuss." The boys look furious at being made to leave, but do as they're told. Once the door closes, I take my seat again. "Makenna, have you thought about who your Underbosses are going to be? You have Connecticut, Philadelphia, DC, and New Jersey."

I hide my grin, those fucking bastards doubted me and they paid the price. Nobody undermines me and gets away with it.

"I have for Connecticut, and Philly, but not the others."

He nods in approval, "Who have you in mind for the job?"

"Romero for Connecticut as he's marrying Holly, it'll be his wedding gift and Finn for Philly."

Granda's grin spreads across his lips, "I agree with both of them. What about Pat and Cian?"

I scoff, "Why would I have anyone working below me that I don't trust to have my back?"

Now it's Da who grins widely. "I wouldn't have anyone work for me that I don't trust."

Granda nods. "Okay, well maybe think about having two of your men move up the ranks."

"Yeah, I'll think about it. I have a few in mind," I tell him absently. I had wanted to ask Patrick and Cian but that shit's not going to happen any time soon. If they want the position, they're going to have to work for it.

Shouting pulls us from our conversation and I'm on my feet and moving toward the door. When I open it I see Patrick and Cian standing on one side of the room and Finn, Danny, Dante, Romero, Alessio, and Killian standing on the other. It's like they're having a stand-off.

"You two are a fucking joke," Finn growls. "What you said to her in there was out of fucking line. She's our sister."

"What the fuck did you say to my wife?" Dante demands moving past Finn and stalking toward Patrick and Cian. "What. Did. You. Say. To. Her?" He clips out each word.

"Enough!" Granda yells and I walk toward Dante, needing to touch him. "This shit isn't going to happen anymore. Your father and sister are the Bosses. You have a problem with that, come to me about it. You ever show the disrespect I saw in that room again, I'll see to it that you'll disappear from the face of the earth. Do I make myself clear?"

Both of them nod, looking contrite. Stupid fuckers.

Dante pulls me into his arms and I place my hand on his chest, feeling the beat of his heart beneath my fingers, loving the way it settles me. "You okay?" he asks quietly.

"We'll talk about it later," I assure him as I tighten my arms around him. I lift my head so that I can see his face. "Thank you for not killing my brothers."

His lips twitch, "It's only fair, you restrain the urge to kill mine on a daily basis."

I can't help but laugh at that, "That is true." I pull out of his arms but instead of releasing me, he leans down and captures my lips, giving me a long, hard kiss.

"Jesus Christ," Finn mutters. "Get a goddamn room."

"Everyone sit," Granda instructs us.

I can't keep the smile from my face. I reach for his hand and pull him toward the sofa. He keeps his hand in mine as we sit.

"As you all know, between Da and I we run the Irish on the east coast. What you don't know is that I have a few vacant Underboss positions."

Danny chuckles, "That's because you've killed them."

I glare at him, "I have four vacant positions and I'm filling two of them. Romero is marrying Holly and therefore he'll be my Underboss of Connecticut. Finn, you'll be my Underboss of Philly."

I watch as my brother's eyes widen before he grins. "Fuck, Kenna, I'm honored."

I smile and give him a nod. I knew he'd be the one for the job.

"Who're the other two positions going to?" Patrick asks, a hopeful gleam in his eyes.

"Not you two fucking pricks," Dante snarls and I place my hand on his thigh, trying to soothe him. The last thing we need is bloodshed.

"You and Cian will be working for me, you have six weeks to show me that you deserve to be made Underboss. You'll do whatever the hell I tell you and you'll do it without a fucking complaint. If you so much as disrespect me or Dante, there will be blood spilled."

They both nod and I see the guilt in their eyes, they went too far in Da's office and it's going to take a while before I'll be able to forgive them. Today has been a hell of a fucking day and I can't wait to get home and crawl into bed beside Dante.

"Now that's sorted out, your brother is outside waiting. Danny, go let him in," Granda instructs him and turns to Finn, Patrick, and Cian. "Denis, Danny, and Malcom are Bosses. Remember that." Granda's voice is hard.

"Piss me off anymore today and I'm going to lose my temper," I warn them, the anger of what happened in the office still on the surface. Dante's hand goes to my nape where he begins to massage it. Instantly my anger starts to diminish.

"I'm sorry for what I said, I was way out of line," Cian begins and Dante's hand tenses on the back of my neck. "It's been a fucked up few days and I shouldn't have taken my anger and frustration out on you."

I nod. "Apology accepted." I don't turn to Patrick, if he were to apologize now, I wouldn't accept it, it would just be because Cian did.

I turn my head toward the door when I hear footsteps. I get to my feet when I see Holly step into the room, she looks nervous and I'm wondering if it's because she's meeting the family or meeting her future husband?

I embrace her and she pulls in a sharp breath. "You're fine. Don't stress," I whisper in her ear so that only she can hear me. "Deep breath and hold your head high."

"I'm just scared," she confesses. "I'm moving here. Leaving everything I know behind and getting married to a man I don't even know."

My arms tighten around her. "You're strong, Hol, you've got this. It's not like you're never going to see your family again. Besides, you'll have me here."

"That's the only reason I agreed," she tells me as we pull away from one another.

I'm instantly swept into a hug from Denis and I squeeze him tightly. From the age of thirteen he was the one that kept me sane. He made sure that I was safe and when things got tough he was there as a shoulder to cry on. He was the one that trained me to become Boss and he was there to celebrate with me when I finally did become one.

"Good to see you," he sighs as he lifts me into the air. "I'm sorry I missed the wedding."

I laugh as he puts me down on my feet and releases me. "Eh, you didn't miss much. It was fairly uneventful."

Dante's chuckle sends heat throughout my body. "That it was, babe."

Denis' gaze finds my husband and his eyes harden. "You must be the Italian?"

I step backward and Dante's hand clamps down on my waist. "Yeah, you're Denis," he grunts, no doubt pissed off at being called the Italian.

"Enough with the pissing contest," Granda says. "We've things to discuss."

Malcolm walks up to me and kisses my cheek, he's got a big smile on his face. It's been a while since we've seen each other, a year, maybe longer. He lives in Spain and spends the majority of the year there. He goes home to Ireland once a month for a weekend but the past year, whenever I was in Dublin, he was in Spain and whenever he was in Dublin, I was here in the US.

"Hey, it's nice to meet you," he says to Dante, not an ounce of hatred in his eyes.

I relax against my husband's hold and his hand tightens on my waist. "Same," he replies, his voice not as tight as when he spoke to Denis.

"You must be Romero," Denis says and I turn to look at him, he's one pissed off man right now. His arms are crossed over his chest as he takes in my brother-in-law. If I thought he was rude to Dante, he's downright belligerent to Romero.

"Yes," Romero replies, meeting his gaze.

I tug Dante's hand and return to the sofa, this is between Romero and Denis, no one else will be getting involved.

"Why don't you three go to my office and talk?" Da suggests when neither man says anything. They're just staring at each other. I'm impressed. Romero's holding his own just as I knew he would.

We all watch as Holly, Romero, and Denis move to Da's office. Once the door is closed, the chatter starts up. "So what have I missed?" Malcolm asks with a grin.

"Since Makenna's been married she's not killed anyone. I miss the bitch," Danny says with a grin and I can't hold back my laughter.

"Actually, she killed at least four men at her wedding," Alessio informs everyone and Dante stiffens beside me. Guess he didn't know that.

"Only four?" Malcolm quips as his lips twitch. "You're slacking, Kenna." He shakes his head in mock disgust, causing me to smile. God, I've missed these guys.

"I've actually been good. I've managed to hold off on killing my brothers along with Dante's. For me, I'll call that a success," I say with a grin.

Dante throws his head back and laughs, "Yeah, she's managed to quell her bloodlust."

"As have you," I respond immediately.

"Jesus Christ, you two are a couple made in hell," Malcolm grouses.

Da chuckles, "That's what I told him before he married her."

The door opens and Holly walks out, her body not as

tight as it was when she went in. Romero and Denis walk behind her, Romero with a stupid smirk on his face and Denis with a scowl.

"Holly, you're excused," Granda says and she nods before leaving the room. "Now, it's time to get down to business. Matteo Bianchi is going to die."

Everyone in the room grins. This is what we've all wanted. Every single person in this room hates that bastard. I know that Dante wants to do the honors and I'm going to ensure that he gets to do just that.

SIXTEEN

Dante
___

ENTERING THE CLEARING, the cold air hits us and cuts through me. I'm surprised at just how many *made men* the Irish have. There has to be hundreds here. Makenna is the only woman and yet as she walks past her men, they stand taller, the respect is clear. She keeps her head held high as we walk ahead of her father and Denis. Henry walks ahead of us as Malcolm and Danny bring up the rear, Romero, Alessio, Finn, Patrick, and Cian are in the crowd. Henry wanted them dispersed so that if anyone had any problems they'd be on hand to deal with them.

When my father dies, I'll be having a meeting very much like this one. I'll be making sure to get rid of the naysayers and the doubters. The Famiglia have many men that would kill to take the reins. They'd betray the family if it meant they could lead. They're the ones I need to get rid of and I will. I want to kill my father, not so that I can lead the family, but to get rid of the cancer that he is. He went too far when he ordered the hit on my wife, a hit that nearly killed me too. Makenna has managed to survive both times he's tried to have her killed. I'm not sure she'll survive the next. Although, there won't be a next time. I'll end him, before he touches a hair on her head again.

We've still not come to an agreement on how to kill him. Romero and Alessio want it over and done with quickly, whereas, the rest of us want him to die slowly and painfully for what he did to Makenna. I've seen Makenna researching drugs and shit; knowing my wife, she's going to come up with a way to keep my ass clean.

"Gentleman, thank you for coming today," Henry begins as he takes center stage so to speak. He's standing in the clearing facing his men. Seamus, Denis, and Malcom on his right, Makenna, Danny, and I on his left. Henry himself told me that I was to be standing upfront with them. That I'm now part of the family and when we have meetings with the men, we're a united front.

"You've heard the rumors, well I'm here to set them straight." He continues and he's got the audience's full attention. "We are expanding. We're going to move into the Midwest and once that's done, we're going to move to the west coast. There'll not be a single inch of the US that we don't fucking own."

Makenna smirks as her Granda nods his head to her. "That means gentlemen that there's opportunities for you to rise through the ranks. We're going to need Underbosses for when we take over the rest of the USA. Those that stand with us will be rewarded. Those that go against us," she smiles brightly, "well those motherfuckers will realize what it means to betray the family. Their blood will be spilled."

She squeezes my hand letting me know that I'm free to talk. "As you're aware, I married the badass that is your Boss." Makenna and her brothers laugh at my words. "I'm also your Boss, and when I take over as the head of the Famiglia, she'll be their Boss too. Times are changing, our union is only going to make our families stronger. Anyone who has a problem with who I am or what my wife and I are doing, then I encourage you to be a man and step forward."

The murmuring begins as the men start to talk among themselves. No doubt wondering what's going to happen if they step forward and go against us. After a couple of minutes three men step forward.

"Speak, Thomas," Makenna demands and the man flinches at her harsh tones.

"Boss," he starts, his voice unsure and trembling. "We don't need an Italian fucker to lead us. We're Irish, we have pride." He sneers in my direction and I glare at him.

"Yes, we have pride, we also have fucking respect," Makenna fires back. "That is my husband you are talking about, the man that is going to rule with me."

"Eric, talk," Makenna tells him as she leaves that other fucker standing there wondering what's going to happen to him. I glance to the man on my right.

"Boss, I'm just not sure if joining forces with the Italians is the right way to go." He's softly spoken, like he's talking to a friend, trying to get her to see reason. It's not going to work.

Makenna turns to her father, dismissing Eric.

"Michael, speak," Seamus says, and I turn my attention to the left where a man is standing alone.

"Boss, I have been with you from the beginning. You have had my trust and loyalty from the get-go. But this? A woman leading us." He shakes his head in disgust and I'm itching to move forward and snap his fucking neck. No one disrespects Makenna. Ever. "A woman..." he spits out. "Has no place here."

"Anyone else have a problem with my granddaughter being the fucking Boss?" Henry asks, his voice booming as he does. No one says a word. "Clinton, tell me, what do you think of Makenna Bianchi?"

The man in question steps forward and holds his head up high. "The Boss is someone I respect, sir. She has my loyalty and in turn, I know that she has my back if things get tough. She's a hard but loyal Boss and I for one am happy to have her lead us." Every man in the clearing, except for the three fucking bastards, nod in agreement.

"Makenna," Henry says and she steps forward. "Deal with this."

"Yes, sir." She steps toward Michael and I watch as he swallows harshly. The men around him move away, like he has the plague. Not wanting to be associated with the traitor. Michael's gaze is focused on her face and that's where he makes his mistake. While he's watching her face, she's unsheathing the knife from her boot and within seconds she has her knife at his throat, cutting him from ear to ear. The look of shock on his face makes me smile. He should never have underestimated her. The blood pours from his throat as he slumps to the floor.

"Finn, Romero, deal with the other two idiots," she instructs and they move in sync. Within seconds, they've killed the two men. "I have two Underboss positions to be filled. There will also be more as we take over the US. I'll remind you once again, that if you are not with us, you're against us, and that is betrayal. One that you'll pay for with your life. If you're loyal, you'll be rewarded."

She steps back beside me and I take this opportunity to speak again. "We'll be watching you. There's nothing that you can hide from us. If you need help, come to us. If we find out you've fucked up and haven't come clean, the consequences will be harsh."

The men stand taller and relax somewhat. They glance around at each other and the air feels lighter. Good.

"Let me introduce you to the new Underboss of Philly," Henry says and motions for Finn to step forward. The men cheer and I see that he has a lot of respect from the men. That's good, he'll be a good Underboss. "In two months, my great-granddaughter Holly will be making our Italian connection stronger. She'll be marrying Romero Bianchi and in turn Romero will be the Underboss of Connecticut."

Cheers once again sound, not as robust as when Finn was announced but still they're welcoming. It shows us that they're willing to accept us. I just hope that when it's the other way around, our men will be just as tolerant. When my father meets his demise, there could be an uprising. We're gearing up for it in fact. If the men find out he's been murdered they'll want blood, they won't stop until they find out who killed him. Just the way it should be.

"Now that you've met your new Underbosses, go out and do us proud," Henry tells them. "You know what to do and remember, we're always watching."

With that last threat echoing, Henry motions for us to follow. However, Makenna and Seamus stay behind. These are their men. They want to talk to them.

"You need to greet them, Dante. They're yours now too. It's time to get to know the men that you're leading," she whispers as we walk toward the crowd.

"Boss," an older gentleman says as he comes to stand in front of us, I shake his hand after Makenna does. "Thank you for meeting with me."

Makenna nods, "Of course, Lawrence, what's wrong?"

He sighs, "The shipment was intercepted last night."

I feel Kenna tense beside me. "Where?"

He shakes his head, "They didn't make it across the state. I have the men working on it. I'll keep you apprised. I just wanted you to know what happened."

She nods, but I know that she's not happy. Her body is still wound tightly.

"Congratulations on your nuptials," he murmurs shaking our hands again and shuffling away.

Before I can ask her what the hell that conversation was about an elderly gentleman approaches with a younger man at his back.

"Michael," Kenna says with a smile. "I apologize for making you wait this long."

The name clicks, this is the man that was at Killian's house and she told him to come back with his son.

The old man waves her off. "Makenna, it's fine. I know how busy you are at this time. It's just that, I don't have much longer."

Makenna holds up her hand, "I know, Mike. It's okay, Jason will take over from you."

The relief in both the older and younger man's eyes is clear to see. "Thank you," they say in unison.

"You've been a big part of this world, Mike. You've shown your loyalty on more than one occasion and I know that Jason has as well, if you weren't dying, Jason would have been up for a different Underboss position. We'll make the transition soon, making sure that the men know that just because Jason is your son, doesn't mean he's not the right man for the job."

"Thank you," Jason replies, his hand clamped on his father's shoulder.

"Before you go," Makenna's voice lowers significantly and both men lean in closer. "What have you heard about the shipment that didn't make its arrival to Lawrence?"

Jason frowns, "Nothing, none of the men have said anything."

Michael sighs, "We'll look into it. We sent fourteen

shipments out, Makenna, and we never heard that one didn't make its destination."

"Look into it quietly," she instructs and they nod. "Good, thank you for coming today and Jason, the next meeting of the Underbosses, I'll introduce you."

He gives her a small smile and a sharp nod. "Thank you, Boss."

They shake our hands and follow where Lawrence left.

We talk to a few more of the men before making our way out of the clearing and into the waiting car. Romero and Alessio are sitting in the back and by the looks of things are arguing.

"What are you two arguing about?" Makenna asks as we get into the car.

Romero sighs, "It's just a disagreement."

"About what?" Her tone brokers no arguments.

"Fuck," he growls. "Alessio wants to do it tonight to get it over and done with."

I clench my teeth, I can't believe this shit. Fucking arguing over who kills our father and when.

Makenna glances at me before she looks back at the road in front of her. Her face is flushed and the grip she has on the steering wheel is making her knuckles turn white, not to mention the anger that flashed through her eyes before she turned away. "And you? What is your take on this? I mean, you've made it clear that you want it to be a quick death," she asks and I'm impressed at how she always manages to keep an even tone.

"While I'd love to kill the bastard sooner rather than later, I'm not stupid. I'm under your thumb now," Romero sneers.

I turn and pin him with a stare. "Is that what you think? You don't see this as an opportunity to fucking be the man you should have been? Don't fucking talk to her like that again. She's your Boss, fucking show some respect."

If you had told me weeks ago that the woman I was going to marry would be a stone-cold killer, I would have laughed in your face. If you had told me that I'd fucking love her psychotic side, I'd have shot you in your kneecap. But the truth is, I wouldn't have Makenna any other way. This life we're building, the empire we're creating, it's going to be magnificent, and when it's done, we're going to be unstoppable. The Italians and the Irish together and better than ever.

"You're right. I'm sorry," he says quietly but the sincerity is there. "I'm just not sure about marrying Holly. She's a little…" He drifts off and I know he's not sure what to say, he doesn't want to insult his soon-to-be-bride, but also, not disrespect her.

"Look, Romero, Holly and I are as different as night and day. She's the light to my dark and the good to my evil. Having said that, she's not a saint and she won't claim to be. Holly knows a hell of a lot more about this life than most and she'll be there by your side through the thick of it. If you let her, that is."

He doesn't say anything and Kenna lets him be. "Also, there is only one person killing that bastard of a father of yours and that's Dante. When he does, it'll be done when there's no blowback. No one can know that he did it and if I find out anyone has said a fucking word I'll kill them."

I stare at her, she has a smirk on her face. "You've already figured out how to do it, haven't you?"

She nods, the smile growing wider. "Yeah, we're going to sit down with your father at a restaurant, all of us. It's going to be public and you're going to inject the fucker with Potassium Chloride." She turns to face me and her beauty is breath-taking. "Instant heart attack. By the time the EMT's arrive he'll be dead."

I'm speechless. She's got it worked out completely. Not only will everyone around us believe it'll be a heart attack, the rest of the world will too. The plan is perfect.

"Holy fuck, Kenna." Romero smirks, "Damn, remind me not to get on your bad side."

She grins, "You're safer than most, Romero, or you will be when you marry Holly. I don't kill family."

"I thought you said you had killed your family before?" Alessio comments and I remember that conversation, she was talking to Romero, telling him to embrace his inner darkness or some shit like that.

"I have. I've killed women who have betrayed the family. Women who are married into our family." She sighs, "For some ungodly reason, men seem to think killing women is an act of sin or some shit. I have no fucking idea, we're as lethal and vindictive as men are, hell even worse as we're sly about doing it. So whenever women needed to be killed, I was brought in, especially when it was family. Just a shame that bitch Zoe hasn't done anything. I'd have taken delight in making sure that fucker was burning in hell." The darkness in her voice has my cock straining against my pants.

"Who's Zoe?" Romero asks.

Makenna smirks, "Oh, that's your soon-to-be mother-in-law."

I hold back my laughter at the look of horror on my brother's face. If Makenna hates the woman there has to be a good reason. Romero doesn't have as much restraint as Kenna does and if Zoe irritates him, she's going to know about it.

"Good luck, bro. By the sounds of it, you're going to need it," Alessio chuckles.

"Dante, set up the dinner with your father for next week. We don't want to have it sooner in case the fucker gets suspicious. Besides, I'm going to need to get my hands on the potassium." I nod and she glances in her rear view mirror. "Romero, I need you to do some digging. My drugs come from various different places, depending on what it is and where it's going. Last week I had a shipment come from Canada to Maine where it was sorted and distributed into trucks to bring to my men. Apparently somewhere along the way a shipment went missing. I want you and Finn to find out what the fuck happened. I want to know if it was sent out and if it was, where it was intercepted or delivered."

Romero nods instantly, "Yes, Boss. How much are we talking?"

"Street value of six-point-three million dollars," she replies angrily and now I know why she's fucking pissed.

"On it, Boss. I'll call Finn tonight and we'll find out." He assures her and I watch as the tension starts to seep from her body.

Once we're home, I'm going to take her to our room and strip her out of her clothes and worship her body slowly. My cock is hard as stone and I know that it's not going to be gentle, then again, it never is between us. Our passion runs red hot and it shows in our love making.

SEVENTEEN

Makenna

THE WATER CASCADES down my body, taking the dried blood from my hands. It's almost as if I'm washing away my sins. Killing that arsehole in the clearing was easy. A typical male underestimating me, he just looked into my face and was so zoned in, that he didn't see me reaching for my knife. The men that I've worked with for years, have respect for me, they know what I'm like and they'll have my back, just as I have theirs. It's the way it's supposed to be and I will not tolerate it any other way.

It's not the first kill I've made and it won't be the last, each time I have to end a life it gets easier. The first kill I had was Kinsley's grandfather, it wasn't an up close and personal kill. It was methodical and planned out. When I found out he died, I threw up, and my entire body was shaking. But it was the right thing to do and it didn't take me long to recover. The next kill came easier, a gunshot to the head and it was over and done with. I didn't throw up that time, but his face stayed with me for a while. He betrayed my father and plotted to take him out. He made a mistake and paid the price.

The bathroom door opens, I don't need to look to know who it is. The cool masculine scent of his aftershave hits me. It's Dante. I hear the rustling of his clothes and within minutes his hands are on my hips, spinning me around so that I'm facing him. His expression is full of worry.

"Dante, I'm fine, I'm used to this," I tell him as I press closer to him. He's come to mean so much to me in such a short amount of time.

"I know, babe, trust me, I know you're used to this. But, Kenna, that asshole disrespected you."

I sigh, I'm not sure how he always manages to get to the heart of the matter. "Yeah, it's always going to be like this. I'm always going to be doubted because of my gender."

He reaches for my face and caresses my cheek. "It's fucking shit, babe."

I scoff, "Please, if you weren't so obsessed with me. What would your thoughts have been when you found out that the Irish Mafia had made a woman their Boss?"

His jaw clenches and that's enough to tell me my answer.

"Yeah, so while it's bullshit, I'm more capable than anyone to run the family. I'll never have everyone's support for the mere fact that I'm a woman. But it just means that I get to kill a lot more people."

He nips at my lip, "No, babe, it means *we* get to kill more people. You're my wife. Mine. No one fucking disrespects you and lives to tell the tale."

His hands start to roam my body and my blood heats as it always does whenever he touches me. "Is it always like this?" I ask breathlessly.

His eyes are dark with lust, "What, babe? Is what always like this?"

"So intense whenever we touch? The need to be with you constantly?" My voice is husky as his fingers trail over my nipples and they instantly pebble from his touch.

"Only with you, Kenna," he tells me as his lips descend on mine. The kiss is hard and full of passion. "You're the only woman that's made me want more. That I've ever gotten hard at the mere thought of and the only woman I've ever loved, will ever love. You're fucking amazing, babe."

My heart melts at his words. I may be a killer, but having Dante love me is something I never dreamed of. I didn't think love was in the cards for me, but I'm taking it with both hands and not letting it go. I'll fight to my death to keep it, just as I know Dante would too.

I lift my hands to his hair. "Love you, so fucking much," I whisper. It's hard to describe just how much this man means to me.

He pushes me against the wall of the shower. Whenever I tell him that I love him, he loses control. His hands go to my ass and he lifts me, and in one move, thrusts his cock into me. "Fuck," he gasps.

My fingers are clenching his shoulders as I steady myself. "God. You're so deep," I whimper. He's not moved; he's balls deep inside of me and the fucker is just standing there. "Please, Dante, move."

He gives me a quick sharp shake of the head. "Perfection," he says, his fingers digging into my ass; they're going to leave marks. "I could stay here for the rest of my life. Deep inside you."

I grind against his cock, needing him to move. It's too much right now. I feel stripped raw, vulnerable as he stares into my eyes. The love and devotion he has on his face is almost enough to make me come undone. "Please, Dante,

I need you to move." I'm not above begging. Not with him. He's my husband, the other half of my soul.

He slowly withdraws his cock from me, just leaving the tip inside me before he slams back into me. My back pushes against the wall and I cry out at the movement. He does it again, the slowness of the movements are killing me, I need more. We've never done it like this before. Even though we're in the shower and he's pinned me against the wall, this isn't fucking, this is making love.

I need more.

"Kenna," he groans as he slams back inside of me. "Fuck, babe, I can't get enough of you. I'll never get enough."

I'm moaning with each thrust, my pleasure building and it's not going to take much longer for me to explode. "I'm so close," I whisper against his ear as I cling onto him.

His thrusts get faster and harder, our grunts and moans are drowned out by the running water. Not that we care, we're both too lost in our love making to give a damn.

My body shakes as I detonate around his cock. I come so hard, that I scream his name. He continues to thrust into me as my orgasm takes over my body. I tighten my grip around him when I come down from my orgasm. "I love you," I whisper and lean my head against his shoulder.

That's all it takes for him to fall over the edge, his hands tighten on my hips and he thrusts into me hard, his body shaking as he fills me with his cum.

"It's never like that with anyone, Kenna," he tells me as he sets me on my feet. "You are far beyond any other woman. You match me in every single way."

I feel giddy like I'm some sort of school girl. But I smile at him and give him a soft kiss, letting him know just how much his words mean to me.

He returns my smile and turns me around so that I've got my back to him, shocking me when he reaches for my shampoo. I stay still and let him wash my hair, it's the sweetest thing anyone has ever done for me, and the most personal. Not only does he wash my hair, he washes my entire body. I have never felt as loved as I do right now.

Once he's finished, I escape the shower not saying anything; my throat is clogged and I'm on the verge of tears. I reach for my towel and wrap it around my body.

"Babe?" he questions as he shuts the shower off.

"Yeah?" My voice hoarse. I keep my head down, not looking in the mirror ahead of me as I don't want to see his face, to see the confusion and hurt in his eyes.

Within seconds he's standing in front of me, he puts his finger under my chin. I don't look up, I can't. He's too close. He adds pressure and lifts my face, and my eyes meet his. "Babe, what's going on?"

I shrug, "I've never had anyone do anything so sweet for me. I've known you for a few weeks Dante and you've already shown me more love than I've ever experienced."

His face darkens but he quickly masks it. "Well, babe, you'd better get used to it. You're the only person who gets this side of me," he growls as he lowers his mouth down onto mine. His tongue sweeps into my mouth and he takes my breath away. It's quick but still amazing. "Your family are assholes, they've treated you like shit for years and it stops now."

I smile at him. He's my protector, my perfect, amazing man. "God, I love you," I tell him and his face transforms with a wide smile.

"Love you too, babe." He lifts me in his arms and walks me toward the bedroom. "Time for sleep, tomorrow is a new day and I've got to have a meeting with my father and the other men."

He sets me on my feet and hands me my pajama shorts and tank top. "What about Romero?" He's now one of my men and we've decided not to tell his father about it as that motherfucker will be dead soon. It's none of his damn business anyway.

"He'll be coming with me. Until that asshole is dead, Romero will act accordingly to Famiglia."

I frown. "Even when he's married to Holly, and he's our Underboss he's still going to be very much part of the Famiglia," I tell him and he watches me carefully. "Having him be our Underboss is a way of strengthening the link between the Clann and the Famiglia. He's still your guy, he's still your brother."

His eyes soften. "I know," he says softly, but I'm not sure he does.

"Have you spoken to him about his upcoming nuptials?"

He shakes his head, "He's been very tight lipped about it all. I'll talk to him tomorrow after the meeting with Dad."

I pull on my pajamas and climb into bed, Dante's just moments behind me. When he climbs in, his arms go around me and he pulls me into his body. "Sleep, babe," he commands and I scrunch my nose up at him, causing him to chuckle. "Go to sleep, I've got you."

I yawn and sink further into his embrace. "Good night, husband, love you." I mumble as my eyes close. It's not long until I fall into a deep sleep.

I WAKE UP TO DANTE'S MOUTH ON MY PUSSY, HIS TONGUE doing things that make my toes curl in pleasure. My fingers tangle into his hair and I tug as I grind against his mouth.

"Damn," he growls and the vibrations of his words against my pussy sends shivers throughout my body.

I release his hair and grab hold of the sheets. "Dante!" I scream as my orgasm crashes through me.

He moves on the bed, positioning himself at my entrance, and thrusts into me. My orgasm is still rocking through my body as I'm clinging to the sheets.

"Morning, baby," he whispers as he fucks me.

I smile at him, he's face soft and his eyes still sleepy, he looks gorgeous. "Morning, darling."

His eyes flash and I realize it's the first time I've called him anything other than Dante. I'm lost in his gaze as I fuck him back, our bodies slick with sweat as we fuck mercilessly. Our breaths coming out in pants as we try and find our releases.

I come screaming his name once again and he groans in my ear as he releases inside of me yet again. It's only going to be a matter of time until he knocks me up. I'm not so sure I'm ready for a baby, but I agree that I want nothing between us. If I get pregnant, then we'll be happy and have our own little family. If I don't, then it's okay as it gives Dante and I longer together to learn everything there is to know about each other.

"Are you going to be okay?" he asks after a couple of minutes and I smile. He's worried.

"Yeah, I'll miss them, but we're going to London next month for Danny's wedding, and then a couple of weeks after that, we'll see them all again as Holly and Romero are getting married." I hate saying goodbye to my family, but I know this time that I'll be seeing them soon. It won't be another six months like last time.

He kisses my lips, "You're going to be busy. Holly wants you to help organize the wedding." He's got a stupid grin on his face.

I groan, "Tell me about it. It was either me or have her bitch of a mother ruin it. At least with me, I'll hire someone to do it and make sure everything's running smoothly and Romero and Holly will get the wedding they want. Whereas, if Zoe had her way, she'd have the big wedding that she always wanted."

His hand splays the base of my back as I rub circles on his chest. "What wedding did she have? She and Denis are married right?"

I nod, "Yeah, they're married. It was a shotgun wedding. She was pregnant with Danny at the time and Denis was furious. From what I've heard, he thinks she got pregnant on purpose to trap him. So he married her in secret. She's pissed about that." I can't help but smile, karma's a bitch and Zoe is destined to get hers soon.

Dante chuckles, "Remind me not to get on your bad side."

I grin, "Keep giving me amazing orgasms and you're golden."

He pulls me on top of him and I straddle his stomach. "Well, baby, you have no problems there. I'm unable to keep my hands off you and that's never going to change."

I move so that his cock is at the entrance to my pussy. "Good, because I'd hate to kill you."

He thrusts into me and I groan. "You love my cock, babe."

I laugh. "True, but I love you more," I tell him sincerely as I move.

"And I love you."

God, how did I get so lucky?

EIGHTEEN

Dante
———————

ENTERING DYNAMITE, the club that we own, I see that most of the men are already here. I sent Romero and Alessio ahead of me, I want them to have their ear to the ground, see if there's any rumblings about a coup. The last thing I need is for my father to be on alert that something may happen. That bastard deserves what's coming to him and the sooner he's six feet under the fucking better.

As soon as my father sees me he motions me to come to him. The smug smirk on his face pisses me off, but I dutifully walk over to him and wait for whatever stupid fucking thing he has to say.

"Dante, it's good to see you can pull yourself away from your *wife*." My jaw clenches at the way he spits wife out, but I ignore it and wait for him to finish whatever fucking tirade he's on. "Those fucking Irish are making us look like fools. They've undercut us on all of our products. I won't fucking stand for it."

I sigh, this shit again? He's known for a long time that the Gallagher's have a better control on the drug trade than we do. He has never done anything about it before so why the hell is he pissing me off by bringing it up now? "What do you want me to do?"

Makenna and I have spoken at length about what's going to happen when I take over. She won't be undercutting us like she does, the price of the drugs will go up and we'll all benefit from it. As soon as my father's out of the picture, things for the Famiglia can only go up with my marriage with Makenna.

"You're fucking married to one of them. Do whatever the hell you have to. Find out whatever the fuck you can about the business."

I scoff, "Oh and how am I supposed to do that? Hmm, it's not as though Makenna is in the know."

Oh how untrue that actually is; if my father found out who was truly running the show he'd have a fucking conniption. My father's old school. Women are supposed to serve men, do whatever the hell we want them to. And in my father's case, beat the shit out of them any time he wants in order to keep them in line.

He steps closer to me, getting in my face. "I don't give a fucking shit. I want to know what the hell those fuckers have. I want what those fuckers have."

He's an arsehole, I can't believe this shit. "Whatever," I reply, knowing damn well that I won't be telling him fucking shit. "Have you got Kurt on this too?" I hide my smile when his eyes flash with anger and his back straightens.

"Kurt's currently lying low." Oh I fucking bet he is. "He's in trouble with the law again. Fucker can't keep out of trouble." He shakes his head in disappointment, and I know what he really means, Kurt's lying low so that he won't rat my father out about the shootings at my wedding. "Where are those useless, no-good brothers of yours?" he asks, glancing around the room, as if seeing if he can locate them.

"They're here, they have been for a while," I answer. I saw them as soon as I walked in the room. It's another reason why my father is fucking shit at being the Boss, he's too wrapped up in his own business to be on the look-out for danger.

He glances around the room once again and I see the exact moment when he sees them. "Fucking Romero," he mutters and I turn to see my brother with a glass of whiskey in his hand. "Can't that motherfucker do as he's told once in his fucking life?"

"He's having a drink," I say as I scan the room. Everyone's here now and they're milling about as they wait for my father to get his shit together and speak to them.

"He's useless, he'll never amount to anything," he says through clenched teeth. "He's always been useless. He's no good for the Famiglia, and he's only here because he's my *son*." He spits out the word son as though it leaves a bad taste in his mouth.

How the hell did we not kill this motherfucker before now?

He turns and walks up the steps to the balcony, and like a fucking asshole he towers over us, like he's some fucking king. "Gentlemen," he says loudly, cutting through all the murmurs from the other men. "Welcome."

I roll my eyes at his dramatics, he thinks he's the fucking Godfather.

"Those Russian bastards are still on the loose, how close are we at finding them?"

Makenna and Romero have been trying to find out where the fuck those assholes are lying low. We keep hitting dead end after dead end. Not only that, they haven't been able to find out how Kurt managed to tip them off about our wedding.

"Nothing yet, Boss, we have all the men on it. They're going to turn up sooner or later," Angelo speaks up. He's one of my men, he's loyal to me and I know that when the time comes he'll have my back.

"Well keep your eyes open and ears peeled. Those fuckers can't have gotten far." The men nod at my father's words. "Okay, now does anyone have anything they need to say?"

I grit my teeth, this is where all the fucking bullshit starts. Any indiscretions between our men that haven't been solved come out here to be resolved and if they can't, then it usually ends with one or both men lying in a pool of blood.

Francesco steps forward, his eyes on me, glaring at me. "Yeah, I want to know why the fuck he married that Irish puttana?"

I grit my teeth and look to my father, even though I want nothing more than to wrap my fingers around his neck and squeeze the life out of him. My father nods, giving me permission.

I step forward and the men behind Francesco take a couple of steps backward, not wanting to be associated with the man that's about to lose his life. Francesco's eyes widen as I get closer to him and he glances around and realizes that he's alone. "What did you call my wife?" My anger is vibrating through my body.

He visibly swallows and he's no longer able to meet my gaze.

"What did you call my wife?" I growl as I step up to him.

"Answer him, Francesco," my father demands and I glance up just in time to see him smirking.

"Your wife is a whore, she's an Irish whore," he tells me as he stands up taller.

Romero shifts in my peripheral vision but makes no move to come to my aid. I don't need him. The way I'm feeling right now, I'd tear every man in this room apart with my bare hands. "She is no whore. She is my wife." My teeth grind together as I clench my jaw.

He fucking shrugs as though it's no big deal. "She was part of the deal."

I lift my hand to his neck, my fingers grip his throat and tighten around it. I relish the feel of his pulse fluttering widely beneath my grip. Within seconds his face is bright red as he struggles to breathe. I take pleasure in that too. "She is not a fucking whore," I growl low. "And you'll die for calling her that."

It's a hell of a lot harder to kill someone this way compared to shooting them, but with the rage I'm feeling, my bloodlust won't be settled until I break his neck. A couple of minutes later, the fucker's lifeless body is at my feet.

"Anyone else have a fucking problem with my wife?" I demand as I glance around the room and my men are shaking their heads a look of disgust on their faces as they stare at the motherfucker on the floor.

"Get the fuck out of here." My father yells, "All of you."

The men don't need to be told twice, they make a hasty exit. I'm right behind them, Alessio and Romero hot on my heels.

"Dante, we'll see you for dinner in a few days," my father says as I reach the door. My steps don't falter and I don't look back, I just nod and carry on walking.

Just a few more days and that asshole is out of our lives for good.

"Bro," Romero says carefully and I don't want to hear it. "You fell into his fucking trap."

"I know," I snap. I know damn well that he fucking set that shit up. He wanted to know how I felt about my wife and I fucking showed him.

"To everyone else, you killed a man who disrespected you. But to our father, you showed him that your loyalty is now to your wife," Romero says and shakes his head. "We've got to watch your back."

I groan, great, just what I fucking need right now. "Don't fucking tell Makenna."

Romero chuckles, "Yeah, I'm not going to be the one to inform her that her husband may now be on a hit list. Good luck with that."

I glare at him, "I'm not telling her either. She doesn't need to know."

"She's going to kill you if you keep it from her and she finds out. She's going to have your balls," Alessio says finally entering the conversation.

He's right, but I don't tell him that.

"No one tells her anything," I reiterate. I know her; if she finds out that my father is going to fucking kill me, she'll off the bastard herself.

"If you say so," Romero says as we reach my car. "I'm warning you now, when she finds out, I'm immigrating."

"YOUR FATHER IS AN ARSEHOLE," MAKENNA GROWLS AS soon as she walks into the house.

I raise my brow, she didn't even say hello. "What's he done now?"

"Like you don't know. For fuck's sake, Dante. Why the hell are you acting as though you have no idea what I'm talking about?" She glares at me and I turn to Romero and Alessio, wondering which one of those assholes told her. "Don't worry, your brothers didn't tell me. You should know by now, that I know everything."

I narrow my eyes, "You have a fucking rat in the Famiglia?"

She doesn't deny it, "Dante, when the hell were you going to tell me? Hmm? When your father made his first attempt? Dante, that man has tried to kill me twice already. The next time he may get lucky."

"He's not going to fucking kill you, nor is he going to kill me. We're going to make sure that he dies before he even gets a chance."

She doesn't answer me, instead, she reaches for her laptop and sits on the sofa. She types away on the fucking thing and I'm about ready to pull my damn hair out. How the hell can she make me so fucking mad without saying a word?

"Romero, when you and Holly get married would you prefer your own house or would you like to stay in the new house with us?" she asks him, not once looking up from her laptop.

He glances at me and I shrug, it's up to him to make the decision. It's a two and a half hour drive from New York to Connecticut so he could stay with us and commute whenever he needs to go there. A lot of Underbosses live in New York, but rule over a different state.

"Have you spoken to Holly?" he asks her and finally she raises her head and the look she gives him would make a lesser man cry. "What?" he asks irritably.

"Why don't you ask her? She's going to be your wife," she snaps and seems as though we're all going to be dealing with my pissed off wife today.

"I don't have her number," Romero confesses quietly.

Makenna reaches for her phone and after a few seconds, Romero's cell beeps. "There, now you have it. Ask her where she'd prefer to live. Alone with you, or with your arsehole brothers?"

"Babe?" I sigh when she glares at me. "Want to tell me what's wrong?"

She scrunches her nose up as though I'm amusing her. "Are you really that thick?" Her Irish accent is getting thicker with each word. "You didn't tell me because you didn't want me to worry."

I can't deny it, she's right.

"If I were a man would you have told me?" She gives me a pointed look. She's right, if she were a man I would have told her, but she's not and as she told me herself, my father has tried to kill her twice already.

"So while I was out with Kinsley looking at fucking houses for us, you were being irrational and showed your father that I'm more than a wife in name and effectively pissed him off. That maniac wants me dead and you've given him even more ammunition to do so."

"Kenna…"

She cuts me off with a glare. "Did it ever occur to you to let me know so that I'd be more vigilant? That maybe, just maybe, your sadistic father would get to you by hurting me because you love me?"

Her words hit me just as she intended them to.

"I see you're finally fucking thinking. Dante, the next time you keep something from me, I'll cut your balls off and feed them to you," she warns me then turns her attention back to Romero. "What did Holly say?"

He grins and it seems like my brother is a little lighter about the whole situation. "She's got a fucking temper."

Makenna rolls her eyes. "She's a redhead and she's fucking Irish. What did you expect?"

His grin grows wider, "She would prefer to live with you for a while. Just until she gets to know me."

Makenna nods, "What she means is that if you hurt her in any way, I'll be close by to kill you." She types away on her laptop, "I've put a bid in on a house. I'm hoping it'll be ready by the time you and Holly are married."

"Already?" I question, wondering how the hell she manages to do so much in less than a day.

She blinks, "Yes, already. I hate fucking sitting around twiddling my thumbs. So while you were off killing the arsehole that called me a whore, I was looking for a home for us. Now do you have any other questions?"

"Yeah," I say and she raises an eyebrow. God, she's so fucking hot when she's pissed. "Did you get the Potassium?"

She puts her laptop onto the table in front of her and I watch as she takes a couple of breaths. "Of course." She sounds insulted that I'd even ask her that. "Everything is set in motion, Dante, all you have to do is inject the bastard."

I walk over to her and lift her off the sofa and into my arms. She holds onto my shoulders to steady herself. "I'm sorry I didn't tell you," I whisper as I walk us out of the sitting room and the fight leaves her body. "I'm going to fuck up, my instincts tell me to protect you at all costs and sometimes I'm going to act before I can think."

"Do it again, Dante, and I'll kill you in your sleep."

I grin as I enter our room. "I'll try not to."

She narrows her eyes at me. "What the hell do you think you're doing?"

I grin, "Oh, baby, makeup sex with you is going to be fucking hot."

She huffs, "Of course it is."

I throw her onto the bed and she giggles. "Let's see just how hot."

Her eyes fill with lust as she watches me strip out of my pants. "Oh, Dante, we should have fucked while we were arguing. I'd say that would be off the charts."

I fucking love this woman.

"Next time, baby," I promise her and I'm rewarded by her soft smile.

God, what did I do in a past life to deserve her?

NINETEEN

Dante

WE'RE HAVING a breakfast meeting with Seamus; he wanted to talk to Makenna and I and see what plans we had. At first Makenna was sceptical, but he wants them to work closely together seeing as they both only want what's best for the Clann. She agrees with him and so do I. As much as her father would like to think that she'd go to him with any problems or ideas that we have, he's not the one she's gonna go to. She told me that she never did before and she won't now. It's what I'm here for, we're a team and we work everything out together.

So far everything he's said has made sense, and I can tell that Makenna is very impressed. He has deals in the works to open new businesses, plus the deals with the Triad on weapons. From what I've gathered the Gallagher's and the Triad go way back, their relationships have been kept quiet and it serves them both well. But when push comes to shove, I wouldn't trust them as far as I could throw them and neither does Makenna or her father.

"The shipment will be in on Monday," he tells us and I know that he's talking about the drugs. Last week,

Makenna told him her concerns about the drugs going missing and we've set up a fucking sting to see if it'll go missing again.

She nods and my jaw tightens, the thought of there being traitors among the men pisses me off. "Good, I want to make sure that the Underbosses know when and where."

Seamus grins, "They will. Don't worry, everything is in place."

"Boss…" Finn says quietly, pulling our attention away from Seamus. I turn to Finn and see his stony expression. He's got a good poker face, that's for sure but when he glances at Romero I realize that they're both pissed off.

"I'll call you later, Da," Makenna mutters as she slides out of the booth; I'm right behind her, throwing money down onto the table. I catch Seamus' smirk before I follow Makenna. I reach her as she gets to the door.

Things between us have been better, especially when I realized that keeping her in the dark wasn't the right thing to do. I was fucking right about make up sex, it was hotter than anything we'd ever done before. So much so that I'm seriously thinking about starting an argument just to see how amazing the sex would be.

"You okay?" she asks, tonight is the night that we go to dinner with my father. That motherfucker is finally going to meet his maker.

"Yeah," I sigh. She's asked me five times already today and it's not even lunch time. "I've got this baby," I tell her quietly glancing around to make sure that no-one can overhear our conversation.

"I know you do. I have complete faith in you, but that's not what I meant." She's worried about how it'll affect me, she thinks I'm going to go crazy after killing my father.

Her hand clasps mine and I give her a reassuring

squeeze. "I'm going to be fine, it's not going to faze me. That asshole has caused you enough pain to last a fucking lifetime," I say as we exit the restaurant. I pull her into my body and hold her close. I love having her body against mine. "I love you, Makenna, and I'm going to do whatever I can to make sure you're safe. This has been a long time coming for that asshole and I'm fucking glad that I'm the one that gets to end him," I whisper in her ear so that no one can overhear us. She wraps her arms around me and holds on tight. "It's all going to be okay. We're going to have everything we've worked for."

She nods, knowing that I'm right. Even though I have had this dread in the pit of my stomach all day.

"Let's go see what our brothers have found. They look homicidal," I comment and she smiles. It's a fucking relief to see both of them getting along. I thought for sure they'd kill each other by now.

I lead her over to Finn's parked car and wait until she slides into the back seat, I'm right behind her. "Talk to us," I demand when Finn pulls into the New York traffic.

"We managed to trace the drugs," Romero says and he has our complete attention. "Michael was right. He sent out fourteen shipments, in fourteen different trucks."

He pulls out a tablet and brings up a video, he passes the tablet back to Makenna and I.

"Okay, so tell me what am I looking at?" she asks not starting the video yet. She wants to know what she's dealing with.

"Did you know that all those trucks have trackers on them?" Finn asks and Makenna smirks. "Of course you did. Hence why you asked us to look into it. You don't want anyone else knowing."

Makenna raises her brow and I bite back my laughter, as Finn clenches his jaw. "Christ, I forgot how annoying you are," he grumbles but there's no heat in his words at all. Of all her brothers, Finn loves her the most. He's protective of her and I can see how much he admires her.

"Finn…" she warns.

He sighs, "Right, so we were able to track the vehicles and none made any stops they weren't scheduled for, when they did stop we were able to find security footage either in the gas station they stopped in, or from across the street."

Makenna glances at me and I can see that she's losing her patience, she wants to know what the hell they've found.

"How about we cut to the chase?" I tell them and they nod.

"Lawrence is an ass and he received the drugs. The fucker unloaded the shipment in broad daylight. We have him read handed; video proof."

Makenna hits play and we watch as the old fucker orders his men around as they unload the truck.

"We have another shipment next week. I want this shit dealt with before that," she says through clenched teeth. "I have to call Granda." She shakes her head. "Fuck. Just what we need right now."

She passes me the tablet and pulls out her cell, she's right, we don't need this right now. We're in the midst of getting ready to take over the Famiglia as well as joining the Clann and Famiglia together. Having a thieving traitor among us isn't great for business. Lawrence will need to be taken care of and soon.

The conversation she has with her grandfather is brief, I guess there's not much you can say. She ends the call. "There's a meeting called for tomorrow morning. Everyone is to be in attendance."

I lean my head back against the chair. These next two days are going to be fucking exhausting. Tomorrow we'll deal with the traitors; we're coming into a new era and it's time to make changes.

"The sooner this week is over and done with the better," Makenna grouses from beside me; she's pissed as hell. "Finn, Granda says next week you'll be taking over Philly. He wants to know if he should put you in contact with a realtor?"

It's less than a two hour commute, so if Finn does move there at least Kenna can see him without having to drive all day or fucking fly halfway across the world to see them. He's silent and I'm surprised, he's usually got something to say.

"Finn, move to Philly. It's not like we're not going to see each other. As much as it pains you, you work for me and that means we'll be in constant contact. If you go to Philly, you'll be able to grow."

Fucking hell. When she cares about someone she really wants the best for them.

"Staying with Da isn't the answer, Finn. As much as he won't mean to, he'll try and dictate what you should do. An Underboss rules. I am your Boss but also your confidante. As is Dante. We want our business, our family to thrive and it's why we want both you and Romero to lead. You both need to step up and show the world that you are both more than just the sons of the Bosses. You need to show them why we gave you the job. Because you're both fucking badasses and you're both more than capable of running the families. But you won't, not unless we die."

"I don't want your job, Kenna. I didn't think I'd be Underboss. But you've given it to me and I'm not going to let you down," Finn says, his voice gruff with emotion. "You and Dante will always have my loyalty and it's not just because you're my sister, though that's a big part of it. I fucking admire you, Kenna, you've been through a lot and come back stronger. You have my loyalty because you give a shit."

Romero nods in agreement. "It's why you have everyone's loyalty. You're not like the others. You show your men that they can count on you which in turn means that you can count on them. Loyalty is earned not given freely and, Kenna, you've earned yours more than anyone."

"Appreciate it," she murmurs and I smirk, she's getting emotional. It's something I didn't think she had in her until the other day when we were in the shower when I saw the fear and love in her eyes. I knew then just how special she was.

She closes her eyes and I know that she's done talking. Tomorrow we'll deal with the traitors. Tonight, we'll deal with the asshole.

I'm pissed. Beyond fucking pissed. My father decided that our 'family dinner' should include his fucking consigliere Pauly. The entire night the two bastards have been making comments about Makenna, I'm barely holding onto my temper. I've been able to restrain from slamming my father's head down onto the table.

Dad's at the top of the table, Pauly to his right and I'm to his left. The way it always is. Kenna's sitting beside me, Romero is seated beside Pauly and Alessio is at the bottom of the table. We're getting more than a few looks, it's not every day that the head of the Italian mafia shows up at the restaurant with his family.

"So, Makenna…" my father begins and I watch as my wife smiles sweetly at him. "How are you liking being married to my son?"

Makenna glances at me and smiles. "I love it. Your son

is the best man I have ever known. I'm a lucky woman." She means the words she says. She really does think she's the lucky one in this marriage but she's wrong. I am. I found my soulmate when I wasn't even looking.

Pauly grins widely as he gives Makenna an appreciative glance and I want to knock that look off his fucking face.

The server brings out Makenna's dessert. I had to stifle my laughter at that. My father hates desserts but Makenna insisted on having one and I wasn't going to tell her no, especially when it was an added bonus of pissing my father off.

She wraps her lips around the spoon as she eats her chocolate cake. I've come to learn that you don't ever come between Makenna and chocolate; she'd gut you where you stand if she found you in her stash. She lets out a moan and her eyes roll back as she eats.

I glare at Pauly who adjusts his pants under the table. Bastard. Makenna gently touches my arm, that's my cue. "You should try some, it's amazing."

I smile as I reach into my pocket, my fingers clasp the syringe. I uncap it just as Makenna feeds me a spoon of chocolate cake, to anyone in the restaurant we're a loving couple, but in fact it is an act. I lift the syringe and shove it into my father's thigh quickly injecting him with the Potassium. His sharp intake of breath is all that I hear as I quickly pocket the syringe again.

"Mm, delicious, babe," I murmur and nip at her lip. Her eyes flare with lust.

She grins at me and turns to face Pauly, "I bet you have a lot of stories you can tell me about my husband."

Pauly throws his head back and laughs, I take this moment to look at my father. His face is pale, he's clutching his left side as though he's in pain and the motherfucker is glaring at Kenna like he wants to kill her. He's unable to say anything as he's struggling to breathe. The potassium is working perfectly.

"So?" Makenna prompts and Pauly laughs harder. "I need you to dish the dirt. I'm guessing he was one of those kids that ran around naked all the time."

Romero and Alessio chuckle at her words, I throw my arm around the back of her chair and my fingers massage her nape. Pauly's looking at us with envy.

"Dante was a very composed child," he begins, throwing a grin in my direction. "He was always sombre except when he was around knives. I knew from the time he was two that he would be a fucking expert at carving people."

Just as a docile wife would, Makenna blanches at his words.

"Pauly," I growl in warning.

Neither Makenna or I give a shit about anything Pauly is saying, we're keeping him occupied enough that he won't glance in my father's direction. Right now, he's sweating and trying to breathe. I've never seen my father look as weak as he does right now.

"It's okay, Dante." Makenna responds to my reprimand of Pauly. "It's your way of life." She frowns. "Oh, Mr Bianchi, are you okay?" The worry in her voice makes me want to chuckle. Instead, I get to my feet, Romero and Alessio right behind me.

"Father?" I question and the asshole helps us by trying to get to his feet and collapsing onto the floor.

"Oh my God. Help us. Please, someone help us," Makenna cries and fuck me, she's putting on a good performance; I'm pretty sure she's got tears in her eyes.

Pauly and I crouch down to my father and Pauly takes my father's pulse. His face pales as he glances up at me and gives me one sharp shake of his head. My father's gone. Makenna's plan worked.

Someone tells us that they've called the EMT's and they're on route. Makenna burrows into my body when I stand up and I pull her into my arms. She's playing her part perfectly. Romero and Alessio are standing on watching, both of their faces etched with worry. Anyone looking on would think that we're a loving family who are worried about their father.

"Dante…" Pauly says, his voice tight. "We can't have them take him to the emergency room. If they get word that he's dead, it could start a fucking war."

"What do you expect me to do?"

He sighs, "We call our doctor, and have both him and the EMT's confirm his death and then we lay him to rest. You're in charge now, Dante. You have to lead."

"Call the doctor," I demand as I push Makenna into Romero and watch as both of them bristle. She's okay being in my arms but not Romero's. I'm not sure why that makes me happy but it fucking does.

The manager moves over to me. "Sir, the EMT's are here," he says quietly.

"Clear the restaurant and let them in," I tell him. He knows us, knows who we are.

"Right away, sir."

Three hours later, we're walking into our home, each one of us sombre as we reflect on the past couple of hours. The EMT's arrived and Pauly informed them of what was happening and they told him it looked like my father had suffered a heart attack. The doctor arrived shortly after and took over, pronouncing him dead and agreeing with the paramedics that it was a heart attack that took him.

Pauly and I had contacted the funeral home and we had

his body moved there. His funeral will be in a few days. We've also spread the word of my father's death and that I'll be the one taking his place. The Capo dei Capi has agreed after Pauly spoke to him. My grandfather hated my father and is probably as happy that the bastard's gone as we are.

"It worked," Alessio says as soon as we enter the kitchen.

Makenna nods, "For now, there's still a few days before we can bury him. Until then, we keep vigilant and make sure no one has any reason to doubt that the arsehole had a heart attack."

"We get it, no celebrating until he's six feet under," Romero says, but he's grinning from ear to ear. "I just want to say, Boss. That was a fucking good plan. Not only that, you actually fucking shed a tear. I was impressed."

She grins. "It all works toward the facade. If we look like a grieving, shocked family, no one is going to look at this as anything other than a tragic accident. Having Dante and I be lovey dovey wasn't a hardship. It put everyone's attention on us and what I was doing with the spoon rather than what Dante was doing with his hands."

I nod, "We keep quiet, act like we're fucking grieving the loss of our father and then when he's six feet under, we can congratulate each other. Until then. No more is said about it."

Makenna leans against me, "Tomorrow is going to be a long ass day. We've got the meeting first thing, but you're all going to have to deal with people wanting to see you, especially you, Dante. You're now the Boss, they're all going to want to ensure their job is safe."

I groan. "Fuck, I hate most of them."

She laughs, "I know, but it's what we do. Are you keeping Pauly on as your consigliere?"

I glance at Alessio and shake my head. No, I'm going

to have my brother take over that position. As though she can read my mind, Makenna nods.

"I'm going to bed," I tell my brothers as I lift Kenna into my arms. "I'll see you both in the morning."

Makenna grumbles, something about her being able to walk but I ignore her and walk toward our bedroom. I need to bury myself deep inside of her and let this fucking day seep away.

TWENTY

Makenna

"HOW MANY OF the men do you think are in on this?" Romero asks as I drive toward the docks. There's an abandoned warehouse out here that we use for meetings sometimes. It's secluded enough that no-one could just come across it, and if they did, we have men guarding it so there would be enough time to get the hell out of there without being seen.

"I don't know, I have no fucking trouble taking the lot of them out." I'm seething. These are my men and they've betrayed me. They've stolen from me and then lied about doing so.

I'm tired. Last night I didn't get much sleep. From the shit show at dinner, along with watching as that arsehole Matteo took his final breath, to having to hang around for hours as we waited for the doctor to do his shit. It's just one thing after another the last couple of days and I'll be glad of the reprieve when we go to London for Danny's wedding.

Romero and Alessio are lighter since their father died, the darkness in their eyes is still there and probably always will be, because their father was an arsehole. I doubt even Dante knows what that monster did to them. Nor do I believe that he or I will ever know.

"Romero," I say after a few minutes of silence.

"Yes, Boss." There's no irritation when he calls me that as I thought there would be, he's become accustomed to it really quickly.

"When Dante and I leave for London, you'll be my eyes and ears. If my men need anything, they are to go to you. You will deal with whatever you can and if you need our help, then call us."

I see Dante's smile from the corner of my eye, we spoke about this last night. With my entire family going to the wedding, we're going to need someone to take the reins and Romero is the obvious choice. Both Dante and I trust him, plus he's more than capable. Dante will be leaving Alessio in charge but will stay in constant contact with him, not to mention he'll have all of his other men on hand.

"Of course, Boss." He replies instantly but I hear the pride in his voice.

"When we get back, Holly will be here. I know you're not exactly thrilled about the wedding and to be honest neither is she. Maybe the two of you can spend some time together and get to know each other before setting a wedding date."

Holly's been upset, she said that Romero is cold and distant and that their marriage is going to be horrible. And while I know that Romero isn't what she described, his outward appearance does warn everyone not to approach. The cold eyes, the disdain in his glare along with the bored, pissed-off look he constantly has. It's his way of keeping people away from him. But Holly is going to be his wife, she's my niece and I want the best for her and that means having a husband who cares about her.

"Yeah, that would be good," he replies and there's a hint of trepidation in his voice.

The car once again falls into silence. I leave Romero, and focus on Dante, his body is tense and he keeps glancing around. He's looking for danger. He's anxious about this morning and I don't blame him, we're going into the warehouse, not knowing who has turned against us. It could be all of my men or it could be just a handful. I hate not knowing.

My da, Finn, Patrick, and Cian will also be in attendance. Alessio will be in the car hidden from view, thanks to my blacked out windows, just in case things go south.

I pull into the parking lot outside the warehouse and see there's already over a dozen cars here. Including Finn's and Patrick's. Good.

"Alessio, keep your eyes peeled. You'll be able to see people as they come in. You're good at reading people, anyone who's acting shady, text Romero," Dante instructs as I slide out of the car. The breeze from the docks hits me and my hair whips around my face.

"On it," Alessio responds quickly.

Once Dante and Romero are out of the car we move toward the warehouse, I notice that Finn is waiting at the door for us.

"Boss," he says in a low voice and I brace for whatever he's about to say. "Lawrence arrived fifteen minutes ago and is acting shady as hell. He's been speaking to a few men and the discussions look heated."

"Thanks, he's not going to go down easy. Everyone who was seen on that security tape unloading the drugs and denies that they did it, dies," I warn him and Romero. "I will not tolerate disloyalty from my men."

They both nod and I look to Dante, he's scanning the

parking lot. God, he's so on edge and it's making me anxious. "Ready?" I ask him and he gives me a terse nod.

Rolling my eyes I move into the warehouse and immediately all eyes are on us. "Is everyone here yet?" I ask loudly and I'm greeted by silence.

"Finn?" I ask needing someone to fucking answer me.

"Not yet, Boss. Michael and Jason are in the parking lot," he replies. "Everyone else is here."

I nod my head in thanks and walk further into the warehouse to where my da is standing. "Morning," I say with a smile.

He grins, "Morning, Kenna, ready for this shit show?" I told him about what Finn and Romero found and he's just as furious as I am.

Commotion sounds by the door and I turn to see Jason helping Michael into the warehouse, the old man walking with a walker, his frail body hunched over as he shuffles forward. "Sorry, we're late, Boss."

"You're right on time," I reply. He's deteriorated a lot since last I saw him. He must be having a bad day today.

"I was informed that a shipment never made it to Miami. Now I know that trip is over two days but we've never had a problem before," I say and watch as unease trickles through some of the men's features. "Michael and Jason personally handle the supplies and having them shipped off. They, along with their men, have never given me any problems."

I watch Michael's men preen at the praise. "Simon," I call out; he's one of the younger men that work for Michael. "How many shipments went out?"

His brows furrows as he tries to think. "Fourteen, Boss. The one to Miami was done first as it has the furthest to go. We always make sure that the furthest ones get shipped off first."

I nod and turn my attention to Lawrence's men. "Peter," I call out and watch as the eldest of Lawrence's men steps forward. "Did you receive the shipment?" I rattle off the date that the shipment was due to arrive.

He doesn't even hesitate. "No, Boss."

I nod just as I did to Simon. "Are you part of the operation to unload the shipment?"

"Yes, Boss, I have been since I've been part of the family."

Well he won't be part of the family much longer. I search the rest of Lawrence's men and see Liam shifting on his feet, he and a few other men look uneasy. "Liam McCarthy." My voice is sharp like a whip. I'm getting angrier the more these fucking bastards lie to me.

"Yes, Boss," he says as he steps forward and Peter takes a step backward.

"Are you part of the operation to unload the shipment?"

He nods, "Yes, Boss."

"Did you unload that particular shipment?" He opens his mouth to say something and I hold my hand to stop him. "Lie to me and your ma will be planning your funeral."

He swallows harshly and I know that it's got to be hard. If he tells me the truth he's ratting on his boss, but if he doesn't he's betraying the family.

"Yes, Boss, I unloaded that particular shipment," he says honestly and I beckon him forward and he moves toward me with trepidation.

"Stand beside Patrick and Cian," I instruct him, then turn back to the other men. "Anyone else agree with Liam? If you do, go stand beside him." I wait and I'm not surprised that half of Lawrence's men come to stand beside Liam and the other's stand by their boss. Okay, we're getting rid of half of them. At least the other half are fucking loyal.

"Lawrence?" I call out, wanting him to answer for himself.

"Those fucking bastards, lying and betraying me. Maybe they're the ones that took that shipment."

Dante shifts beside me, his body humming with anger.

"Last chance for you to change your mind. Pick which side you're standing on, boys."

A few more men move to stand with Liam and I nod to Finn, he'll take note of them and ensure that they're monitored.

"Fine. You have made your choice," I say and turn to Romero. "Play it," I demand and he hits play on the laptop I had Patrick bring earlier on, he's hooked it up to a big projector screen where everyone will be able to see.

As soon as the footage starts playing, my other men move away from Lawrence, not wanting to be standing near the traitorous bastards. The men that stood with Lawrence shift as guilt fills their eyes. They realize they're fucked.

Da's grin can only be described as menacing as he glances at Lawrence. They've known each other for years. Been friends for a hell of a long time. "Why, Lawrence? Why betray the family? Something that you have been a vital part of for so fucking long?"

Lawrence glares at my da, then turns his hate-filled gaze to me and then to Dante. "It was bad enough that I had a fucking woman dictating to me, but I dealt with it, she is your daughter after all. But a fucking Italian? No, I will not bow down to the mutt."

The heat at my back tells me that Dante's had enough, I glance at my da and he's looking at Lawrence like he's never seen him before.

"Gentleman." I turn to Liam and the others that told the truth. "Honesty and loyalty is what this family is about. You have shown everyone in this room that you belong to the Clann." There's nods of agreements around the room. I raise a hand and they quiet down, "As for you," I tell Lawrence and the traitors. "You have shown everyone here that you are not part of this family. You will be dealt with."

The fear in the men's eyes is enough to settle my rage for now. "Anyone betrays the family and they'll pay for doing so. Today you all have learned a valuable lesson. Never betray the family. Never steal from us, and don't fucking lie to us." I continue and the other men in the warehouse nod. They know that Lawrence went too far. We're very lenient in what we allow our men to do. They are free to run their cities as they please, as long as it doesn't reflect badly on the Clann and they are loyal to us.

"You show your loyalty to the Gallagher family and you'll be rewarded handsomely." Da speaks up for the first time, his voice vibrating with fury. "Those who betray us will be treated with the same respect they showed us. Zero. Good luck having your family recognize you."

Both Da and I glance to Dante. It's his time to show why he's the Boss. Da and I have proven ourselves over and over again. Now it's Dante's time to play and he wastes no time in getting down to business. He interlocks his fingers and the sound of his knuckles cracking is harsh in the silence. Romero, Finn, Patrick, and Cian step forward. There's seven men that need to be taken care of. But they're just there for backup, Dante is more than capable of taking care of them.

Everyone is silent as they wait for Dante to make his move. Every single man's eyes are on my husband, anxiously waiting for him to dole out the punishment to the traitors.

Dante doesn't even hesitate, he unsheathed his knife and with a flick of the wrist cuts through the first man's throat. I've never seen him in action before and fuck, he's gorgeous. He moves like he's born to do it as he stabs the next man in the heart. I know how much force is needed to break through the skin and bone to get to the heart and Dante made it look easy.

Heat pools between my legs as Dante effortlessly takes care of the men. He's not even breathing hard as he moves from man to man. I never thought I'd find killing someone be so fucking hot and yet here I am, panting as my husband murders the men that stand before us.

"You don't deserve to have the loyalty of my wife," he growls as he steps up to Lawrence. He's left him for last.

Six men lie at Dante's feet, all dead from various stab wounds. The coppery scent of the blood is heavy in the air, clogging the back of my throat. "My wife is a better leader than you could ever hope to be."

I bite back a smile as a cheer goes around the warehouse. My men are truly loyal and have my back even though I am indeed a woman.

"She'd have died for you and you fucked it up."

Lawrence stands up straighter and I'm itching to end the bastard's life as is my da, but we don't, we stay where we're standing and let Dante deal with him. "You're nothing but an Italian inbred mutt and you'll never have our respect."

Dante shrugs, "I have my wife's and that's all I give a fuck about." He lifts his knife and I watch on in sick fascination as he stabs Lawrence in the eye, blood pools from the socket as he squeals like the pig he is. "You on the other hand will die with everyone knowing that you are a traitor; that you betrayed the family and stole from your Boss." He nods to Romero and Finn and they step forward to hold

Lawrence upright. Dante jabs his knife into Lawrence's other eye and I can't hold back my smirk this time.

"Your wife will be shunned, your sons considered traitors too." Dante informs him and it's true, their father's betrayal will always look bad on them. "You've ruined their lives and they're going to hate you for it." With that parting message, Dante slices through the fucker's throat.

Finn and Romero step back quickly, dropping Lawrence to the floor to escape the blood splatter. Once Lawrence hits the ground, there are cheers and hollers. The men are happy that the traitors are dead.

"We celebrate tonight," I yell above the cheers and the men quiet once again. "We rejoice in the fact that we've rid our organisation of rats. Tomorrow, we work harder than ever."

Michael and Jason catch my gaze, the pleading in the old man's eyes has me nodding. "Gentleman, as you've probably guessed, Michael will not be with us much longer. Jason has more than proven himself capable of taking over. As of today, he will be the Underboss of Maine. Liam, you have two weeks to prove that you can take care of Miami. We'll be watching. Patrick and Cian, you have done well so far. The next few weeks you'll be trailing Romero and Finn as they take over their territories. The next meeting will be held when I return from London."

A chorus of 'Yes, Boss' echoes around the room.

"Dismissed," Dante clips out, he's still pissed.

"Yes, Boss," is once again repeated and I can hear the begrudging respect the men have for him. He took on seven traitors and didn't break a sweat. He's earned the right to be called Boss.

"Da, I'll talk to you later," I tell him as I reach for Dante's hand. "Finn and Romero, you're taking Patrick, Cian, and Alessio with you. You're training them."

"Yes, Boss," Finn replies and Romero nods.

"In a hurry?" Dante questions. As we walk towards our car, Da's calling the clean-up crew to get rid of the bodies.

"Yes. You were fucking hot killing those arseholes," I say, my voice husky and full of need.

Dante chuckles, "Oh, baby, that's how I feel every time I see you do what you do best."

I shake my head. "We're fucking nymphos."

"Yep and I wouldn't have it any other way."

I lean up on my tiptoes and plant a soft kiss against his lips. "Love you," I whisper.

His eyes soften. "Love you too. Now let's go home, I have my husbandly duties to take care of."

I glance back at the warehouse where my da is standing, a smile on his face as he looks at Dante and I. God, my life is amazing. I never thought I could love anyone as much as I love Dante and he loves me harder than anyone ever has before.

I'm looking forward to spending the rest of my life ruling the world with him at my side.

Epilogue

Dante

I HEAR movement in front of me and I glance up at Stefan. I bite back my smile. He's got a white bandage over his nose, green and blue bruises mar his skin under his eyes. He glances at my wife and the respect shines through. It wasn't always like that, but Makenna being Makenna wouldn't and doesn't tolerate any bullshit. When I introduced her to my men and informed them that not only am I the Boss, but she is now as well, there was a hell of a lot of hostility.

Thankfully, Makenna had the foresight to show the men just how capable she was at running the show and we had set up a boxing ring in the middle of the fucking club. Six men went in against her, including Stefan and my best fighter, Danilo. My men were shocked to say the least. When she said she wanted to fight them, they laughed at her. But Christian thinking that he's the shit, climbed into the ring and started throwing jabs. I chuckled when Makenna threw a haymaker and knocked the fucker out.

With each man that went into the ring the rest of the men's respect started to grow. When she had Stefan hitting the canvas, I knew that the men would respect her as the Boss.

When Danilo stepped into the ring, I tensed. He's an animal when he gets into the ring, but he's the best. He started off slow and Makenna dodged every punch he threw. Then he turned up the heat and my wife didn't falter; she took a couple of punches but she gave him back as good as she got. In the end I called a stop to it, it was either that or go into the ring myself and tear Danilo apart for making my wife's lip bleed.

"Boss…" Stefan says and I nod for him to continue. "We have to leave in the next fifteen minutes. I've tried calling the other Boss but no answer."

I bite back my curse, Makenna is pissed at me. Since we've taken over as head of the Italian Mafia, we've had a close team around us. It's what happens to all Bosses but Makenna pitched a fit. She's never had a team and she doesn't want one. It's been a fucking week and we're still arguing over it. Thankfully, the sex is off the charts and making love to my wife is a favorite pastime of mine. The angrier she is, the better the sex.

"Are you and Alex packed?" To appease Makenna, we've mixed the Italians and the Irish as part of our team. She still hates it.

"Yes, Boss, our luggage is in the car and we're waiting for the Boss' luggage."

I get to my feet and sigh, if they're waiting for her luggage then she's not finished packing yet. "We'll be ready in ten," I tell him and head toward the bedroom.

When I walk into the room, I don't see her, though there's a light coming from the en-suite bathroom and the doors slightly ajar. "Kenna?" I question and I'm met by silence. I frown when I push the door open wider and see her sitting on the toilet staring at something in her hands. "Baby?" I ask softly and she turns to face me. I've always known my wife is gorgeous, and I know that she rarely shows her emotions. But seeing the sheer emotion in her eyes makes my knees go weak. She's stunning.

She licks her lips as she glances down at her hands again. "I called Kinsley," she tells me and I listen, not wanting to interrupt, I'm fucking anxious not knowing what's going on. "I needed my girl. I needed her to let me know that it's going to be okay." Her voice is soft and gentle, and I know how hard it is for her to admit that she needed help.

"Baby, talk to me, what's going on?" I beg as I get on my haunches beside her.

"We've spoken about it. We both knew it was a possibility, but I wasn't sure I was ready. We've only known each other just over a month. I thought it was too soon, but I guess it's not."

I'm confused, "You're going to have to spell it out to me, babe, I have no idea what you're talking about."

She smiles and my breath leaves me in a whoosh. God, I'm a lucky son-of-a-bitch to have her in my life. She raises her hand and shows me what she's been looking at. "Kins has said that if we don't have her as Godmother she's disowning us both."

My throat constricts as I stare at the white stick in her hand, the two pink lines so bright, so easy to see. "Fuck," I whisper and she laughs. "You're having my baby?"

She nods. "Yes, I'm having your baby."

I close my eyes and sit down on the floor beside her quickly pulling her into my lap. "Love you," I tell her, needing her to hear my words.

She wraps her arms around me. "I'll stop arguing

about having the team with us," she whispers. "But I don't want anyone to know, Dante. We're known now, the two of us as being the Boss. Taking me out while I'm pregnant would be our enemies best bet. It's not going to happen. So no-one can know."

I agree. "We'll work it out," I assure her, we'll make it work. "We've got to go, babe."

She nods against my shoulder. "Thank God, there's a bedroom on the plane." She kisses my lips and I stand with her in my arms.

"You're insatiable."

She giggles, "Like you'd ever complain."

I'm a man, of course I wouldn't. I'm addicted to her and there's no way I'd ever go without her. "Where's your luggage?"

She scrunches up her nose, "It's behind the door in our bedroom."

Ah that's why I didn't see it. "Okay, grab your purse and whatever else you need. I've got the luggage." I stand up, pulling Kenna to her feet and hold her body flush against mine. As always my cock strains against my zipper. I give her a long and hard kiss, my tongue sweeping into her mouth and dominates it.

She grins when I pull away. "You're happy." It's a statement but I still nod, "Good, so am I. It's going to be an adjustment but we're more than capable."

"Fuck yeah," I reply and she laughs as she pulls out of my arms and drags me into our bedroom. "Time to go." We're flying out for Danny's wedding and Makenna's looking forward to seeing her family again.

"Danny's stressed. He and Melissa are non-stop arguing. I think they actually hate each other." She tells me as we walk down stairs.

"Does her family know she's pregnant yet?" How the

hell they've managed to keep it a secret from them is beyond me.

"No, from what I've gathered, not all is as it seems with Melissa."

I grin, "Oh you mean just as it was with you when I married you?"

She glares at me. "I don't see you complaining. You love me when I let my psychotic side out."

That I fucking do.

"Maybe Danny will get lucky?" She shrugs. "She seems like a sweet girl," she says as she hits the bottom step and turns to face me.

"Time will tell babe. Not everyone is going to be like us."

Her face softens as she bites her lip. "Yeah."

"Congrats, man," I say to Danny as I watch his bride talk to her father. There's something weird about the dynamics for that family.

"Thanks. I didn't think it would happen after this morning."

I frown, Makenna never said anything. "What happened this morning?"

He sighs, scrubbing his hand down his face. "Her family found out that she's pregnant and were furious. Her father and brothers more so than anyone else. But Da talked to her father and seemed to smooth things over. But the entire time, Melissa sat there staring at the fucking wall. It's weird. I don't know what the hell is going on with them but it's not sitting right with me."

"You mean the way that the women treat her?"

He nods, "Yeah, they don't even acknowledge her. It's

fucked up, and she rarely talks to me. I don't know what to do. How the fuck did you get Makenna to talk to you?"

I laugh, "Do you really believe that anyone can make her do anything she doesn't want to?"

He sighs, "You're right."

"Just keep trying, you're married now. Show her that you at least want to try and, Danny, keep your dick in your pants."

He gives me the finger as he turns on his heel and goes to claim his wife who looks as bored as I feel.

Hands wrap around my stomach and I capture them. "Trying to sneak up on me, babe?"

She shakes her head. "No, but I overheard what you and Danny were talking about."

"You know what's up with that family?" She nods and I glare at her waiting for her to spill the beans.

"We're not telling Danny because, well, it's his wife and he should find out himself or let her tell him. She lived with her mom until she was fourteen when she went to live with her dad and his family. I'm not sure what happened for her to move in with them, but it must have been bad seeing as Tanya Harding hates her husband's daughter and treats her like shit. I've come close to slapping the bitch for the way she puts Melissa down."

Fucking hell. "Danny's got his work cut out for him."

She nods, "That he does. Thank God we didn't have any bullshit drama."

I chuckle, "We deal with it by killing people who bring the drama."

She grins wide. "Damn straight."

I pull her into my arms and move her toward the dance floor, and we sway to the music. "We never got to do this at our wedding," she says and I realize that she's right.

"I'm sorry." Fuck, I feel like an ass for not even knowing that.

She smiles brightly, "Don't be, our wedding was a hell of a lot more fun than this is."

I capture her lips and kiss her as the music continues to play.

"God, is it too early to leave?" she asks as she glances around.

"Probably, but we'll make a reappearance later," I mutter but pull her out of the ballroom and toward the stairs, grateful that we booked into this hotel for the night. We make it to the elevator and the doors slide open. I pin her against the wall of the elevator and watch as her chest rises and falls rapidly. Her legs brushing together with need and her pupils are dilated. The elevator dings and I pull her with me and move toward our room.

She pouts as I unlock our door. "My wife has needs and I'm going to see to them."

She waltzes into the room and turns to face me. "Actually," she begins, pulling me inside and closing the door behind me, "it's your needs that I want to see to." She falls to her knees and reaches for my belt buckle.

My cock is encased by her warm wet mouth as she sucks me dry.

"Fuck. Kenna," I grind out, my control gone as my orgasm starts to surface. "Baby, I'm going to come." That doesn't stop her, she sucks harder and faster until I'm unloading into her mouth. My orgasm so intense that my vision blurs.

When I'm able to function again, I lift her into my arms and walk her to the bed. I lie her down lifting her dress to her hips, I'm surprised that she has no underwear on and in one swift movement I thrust deep inside of her.

"I'm going to spend the rest of my life making love to you. Fuck. I love you."

She moans, "I love you too. Now fuck me," she demands and I can't help but chuckle.

"As you wish, my queen."

What's next?

Are you ready for more?
Danny and Melissa's story is up next!
https://books2read.com/UnexpectedUnion

A moment of passion leads to an unexpected union...

Melissa Harding has veered on the side of caution, always keeping her past locked up tight. Until one night she decided that she'd let loose. Which came at a cost. Getting pregnant was shocking enough, but marrying the head of the Irish Mafia was worse.

Melissa hopes that she can keep her darkest secrets hidden. But her new husband has other ideas.

Danny Gallagher never had plans on settling down. His family doesn't have a great track record when it comes to marriages. That is until his new bride's secrets start to unravel, Danny realises that he's finally met his match.

The darkness he has inside burns deep within her.
When enemies start to rise, Danny and Melissa find out just how perfectly matched they really are.

What happens when a traitor has plans to take Danny out? Will the couple be able to find them before it's too late?

All the ways you can follow Brooke.

Website: https://brookesummersautho.wixsite.com/website

Newsletter: https://brookesummersautho.wixsite.com/website/newsletter

Facebook: https://www.facebook.com/BrookeSummersAuthor/

Join Brooke's Babes: https://www.facebook.com/groups/BrookesBabes/

Bookbub: https://www.bookbub.com/authors/brooke-summers

Instagram: https://www.instagram.com/author_brookesummers/

Twitter: https://twitter.com/Author_BrookeS

Acknowledgments

Christine: You are seriously the best! You help so much, I'm not sure what I'd do without you! Thank you!

Jessica F: Just like Christine, you are amazing! You've done so much to help me, thank you!!!

Jessica A: Hmm, what do I say? You know how much I adore you, how bloody amazing you are. ;) I don't want to keep going on, you'll only get a big head. Lol.

Krissy: As always, you've gone above and beyond for me! There are not enough words in this world to describe just how much you mean to me. Love you muchly. You're the best friend a girl could ever have!

Sarah: You are bloody fantastic! Thank you so much for being an awesome beta reader.

And thank you to you, for reading this book.

Lots of Love
Brooke xx

Printed in Great Britain
by Amazon